DEFRIENDED

BY RUTH BARON

POINT HORROR

ISBN 978-0-545-56761-9

Library of Congress Cataloging-in-Publication Data Available

10 9 8 7 6 5 4 3 2 1   12 13 14 15 16

Printed in the U.S.A.   40

This edition first printing, January 2013

The text is set in Adobe Garamond Pro.
Book design by Natalie C. Sousa

For Margot Baron, with love and gratitude.

"It is also the pardonable vanity of lonely people everywhere

to assume that they have no counterparts."

— John le Carré

CHAPTER 1

So bored I think I might be dead. Jason wrote the imaginary status update in his head as Ms. Rowen droned on about the properties of iron. He thought about sneaking his phone from his pocket and posting it to Facebook, but Ms. Rowen had hawkish eyes and no patience for rule breakers. Broadcasting the monotony of chemistry to all 248 of his friends wasn't worth the risk of getting the phone confiscated for the week.

Two hundred forty-eight friends. Two hundred forty-nine if you included the request from his aunt Sally that he'd been ignoring. The list was like a tour through his utterly pathetic middle and high school career. There was Rachel Keller, the curly-haired saxophone player he had slow danced with at Jacob Cooper's bar mitzvah. Sadly, that was pretty much the most action he'd had in the past four years. Alex McCoy, a bespectacled kid he'd bunked with at summer camp, flooded his newsfeed with creepy photos of frogs and other unwitting specimens. Sometimes someone like Suzy Garz popped up, though the charismatic captain of the field hockey team hadn't exchanged actual words with Jason since the fourth grade. Not that he was so unhappy about that — he was pretty sure the inspirational quotes she was posting were from a '90s edition of *Chicken Soup for the Teenage Soul*. Either there or the back of a cereal box at Whole Foods.

Jason's eyes wandered around the room. To his surprise, his best friend Rakesh's face was frozen in rapt concentration. It took Jason a minute to realize it was a phone cradled carefully in his hands that had captured his attention. Rakesh could afford to get his iPhone confiscated — he kept a spare one in his locker for just such an occasion. One of the perks of being among the most popular students at Roosevelt High was that girls (and boys and maintenance staff and teachers) were happy to help Rakesh out on the rare occasion he couldn't charm his way out of a punishment. He had 892 friends last Jason had checked. His wide smile and princely cheekbones populated almost as many photos. Jason knew because he was featured in many of them, but he'd untagged any where you could see light reflecting off his glasses or his hair looked floppy. Which was pretty much all of them.

Jason forced himself to concentrate on Ms. Rowen as she explained the process of oxidization. He couldn't afford to get anything less than a B on the approaching midterm. One of the few advantages to leading the world's quietest social life was that his mother allowed him to do pretty much whatever he pleased so long as he made good grades, but if she had even the slightest inkling he was lying to her, it was only a matter of time before she'd take his car — or worse, his laptop — away. He wasn't intentionally deceiving her. He'd sit down at his computer intending to focus on schoolwork, but when Lacey was online everything else had a tendency to fade into the background.

Lacey. His stomach flipped just thinking about her. She had changed everything with two words. "Hey" and "Jason" were things he heard almost every day, but they weren't usually featured next to a profile picture of a gray-eyed girl with beachy blonde hair. And Lacey was so much more than that, too. Since the first time she'd messaged him six weeks ago, they'd barely gone a day without e-mailing or chatting online, and each time he heard from her he could barely believe his good luck. Like him, she was a nut for indie rock, sending song lyrics or links to old Pitchfork posts on bands he thought only he knew about. She was even learning to play guitar, something Jason spent a lot of time wishing he could do. He'd gotten as far as the cheapest Fenders at Strings, the guitar store in the city, before the tiny tattooed clerk with huge round eyes that made her look like an anime character scared him off by picking up a Gibson and banging out a punk rock riff he didn't recognize, probably because she'd written it herself. Lacey didn't seem like the type to frighten easily, and she had a warmth that was conspicuously absent from the ferocious girls who hung around Strings. She was funny — comparing her spacey English teacher to Ms. Frizzle and calling her friends by rapper nicknames like J Money and Funky Dash. Best of all, she seemed to genuinely like Jason.

He knew he shouldn't exactly be composing the playlist for their wedding — or even changing his relationship status — but it was hard to contain his excitement now that he finally had something to think about in chemistry other than whether the clock was broken.

Suddenly, he felt his hip vibrating and was so surprised he bolted to attention. A few of his classmates swiveled in their seats to see what had startled him, and he sat stone still until Ms. Rowen turned back to the whiteboard. His phone rarely rang during the day. He'd sent Lacey his number a few weeks before, and since then, every time his cell buzzed or beeped his heart leapt into his throat. Unfortunately, a sidelong look to his left confirmed it wasn't worth the excitement. Rakesh did his best to suppress the smile beginning at the corners of his mouth, but when you've been friends with someone since you were both in diapers, you get pretty good at recognizing when they're messing with you.

Jason's pocket buzzed again, and he glared at Rakesh before slowly sneaking his phone into his lap.

Rakesh Adams: Admit it — you think ms. R is sexy when she talks about chemistry like this.

And then the second:

U dream about her reciting formulas 2 u

He was about to respond when Ms. Rowen turned back from the board. He shoved the phone out of sight about half a second before her eyes settled on him. "Is something funny, Mr. Moreland?" she asked sharply.

"Um, no." His voice cracked as he answered. As if opening his mouth in front of his entire class wasn't bad enough on its own.

"So that smile on your face is a product of your general delight to be alive? A celebration of how great it is to be Jason Moreland, boy wonder?"

His cheeks burned, and he kept his eyes trained carefully ahead, but he couldn't block out the snickering around him. "I was just, uh, happy I finally understand the formula." Jason prayed she wouldn't ask him to explain — he had no idea what the notes she had copied there meant. She frowned suspiciously, but before she could humiliate him further, the bell rang. Mercifully, class was over.

Jason and Rakesh both made a beeline for the door. "Dude, why didn't you answer my texts?" Rakesh, with his artfully rumpled gray backpack slung over his shoulder, ran one hand through his wavy black hair and used the other to greet kids they were passing in the hall, all of whom parted as they passed. *Like Miss America*, Jason had observed on more than one occasion. And really, if Roosevelt High had its own pageant, Rakesh would be a front-runner for the tiara. He'd probably even manage to pull off faux crystals and inspire half the guys in school to start wearing sashes. It's not that Jason was jealous — if he had his way, he'd be the one making fun of the contestants from home — but he sometimes marveled at the fact that his parents' choices in early childhood playdates had somehow condemned him to a life as sidekick to the most popular guy in school.

"I can't get my phone confiscated just because you got bored in chemistry."

"Oh, do you need it in case you get an important call from Laney?"

"It's *Lacey*," Jason said defensively. They made their way to their lockers to drop off their oversize chemistry textbooks. As they swung the doors shut, Rakesh plucked a tissue paper flower that had been tucked into the vents at the top. Jason raised an eyebrow. "Did I forget your birthday?" he asked.

Rakesh shrugged. "Oh, you know, every day's your birthday when it comes to Amy Kastle."

They made their way toward the cafeteria, pausing so Rakesh could bump fists with a group of basketball players wearing suits for game day. Jason awkwardly slapped hands with the overly eager Dan Greene and wished them luck against Mason. School spirit, another ritual he would prefer to sit out.

They took their seats at their usual table, and Rakesh steered the conversation back to Jason. "So you and Lacey have graduated to the phone?"

"Not exactly."

"Yo, you need to get on that."

Ignoring him, Jason unwrapped his sandwich. Turkey, provolone, mustard on one slice of whole wheat bread, mayo on the other. It was the same sandwich he'd eaten for as long as he could remember. He bit into it. It tasted like yesterday.

In theory, Jason liked English fine, but then Katie Leigh would open her puckered mouth and say things like "I feel like the identity metaphor of the green light is really prevalent here," and Dave Jordan would cut her off to add his own analysis of the spectacles from the billboard even though they were both supposed to be talking about Shakespeare. Jason wished they had never been assigned *The Great Gatsby* over the summer because it was proof that other people could ruin anything, even a great American novel. But the silver lining was that as long as Katie and Dave's "Who wants to be a Princeton student?" pseudo-intellectual battle continued, Jason could tune out and scribble lyrics in his notebook under the guise of taking notes.

It was all turning gray
It was all turning black
Then you were there
And you keep coming back

These things tend to get ugly
Or so I am told
But now that you're here
Everything's coming up gold

Drive out, see the stars, in the car, we're falling hard
Wake up, feel the sun, touch your hair, see your heart

He'd been writing songs over the past year, but he usually got frustrated and gave up before he could finish them. A day or two after he started, Jason would go back to his work and cringe, crumpling up loose leaf or dragging the docs to his trash for that satisfying springy sound. This one was different, though. The song wasn't ready yet — still too sweet, too tidy, and only half done — but it didn't make him want to burn the notebook he'd scrawled it in. He was going to keep writing until it was perfect, and then he would show it to Lacey. Maybe she would even write the music for it.

He looked down at the page in front of him and drew a box around the line "Everything's coming up gold," tracing the edges several times until the ink bled through to the next sheet. It was a good note to end the song on. He could hear it, repeated several times, in his head. He half listened as Mrs. Granger highlighted relevant themes from the *Hamlet* reading he hadn't done, while one eye rested on the clock. He watched the seconds tick by and waited for the day to end. Like he had yesterday, and the day before that.

CHAPTER 2

Jason caught a tantalizing whiff of his mother's lamb chops before he heard her voice. "Babycakes, is that you?"

"If by *you*, you mean *Jason*," he shouted from the hall, tossing his book bag down at the foot of the stairs. His mom was always using cutesy nicknames that embarrassed him. As if being called "dumpling" in public wasn't bad enough, she used the same terms of endearment to address her husband, Mark. Jason was loath to be too closely associated with his stepdad, a mustachioed real estate agent whose boisterous and borderline slimy personality would fit right in at a used car lot. Jason and Mark got along fine so long as they weren't speaking to each other. But when they had to interact beyond polite dinner table conversation, Mark quickly grew frustrated with Jason's indifference to professional hockey and unwillingness to act like one of Mark's poker buddies. For his part, Jason was reminded of how much he missed his dad, who was always traveling for work.

His mom, clad in black yoga pants and a loose T-shirt, was standing over the stove, tending to a frying pan. "Sweet pea, will you try these and tell me if they need more salt?" As a radiologist at the Oakdale Hospital, Claudia Moreland wasn't some sort of Suzy Homemaker offering Jason fresh-baked chocolate cookies as he did his homework, but she prepared dinner almost every night, and Jason loved her cooking. He speared a thinly sliced potato with a fork and popped it in his mouth, scalding his tongue with oil.

"Hot, hot!" he gasped, fanning his open mouth.

His mom couldn't refrain from laughing. "What did you think was going to happen?"

"You couldn't have warned me?" he asked when he'd finally swallowed.

"You couldn't have noticed you were eating them straight out of a frying pan that's still cooking over high heat?" she shot back. "Now tell me, are they okay?"

"Yeah, Mom, they're great." He grabbed another forkful, and this time blew on it before taking a bite.

"How was your day?"

"It was okay," Jason replied. "The same."

"All right, well, I think we'll eat when Mark gets home. Do you have homework to do until then?"

"Sure, yeah, I'll be in my room."

Jason did have homework, but as soon as his door was shut he logged in to Facebook. The little red "1" at the top of his screen made his breath shorten.

Hi J,

I'm supposed to be studying right now, but I can't make myself open my history book. So instead of working, I keep watching the video you sent me of Stephen Colbert singing "This Year" with the Mountain Goats. Oh. Em. Gee. Are you kidding me? WHERE did you find that? Obsessed.

I think I've watched it like 20 times to the point where I'm singing along and everyone in this computer lab is looking at me like I'm crazy, but I don't even care. If I get kicked out of school for this, it will be worth it because tMG videos are literally my favorite thing in the entire world.

How was your weekend? Did you go out or did you lock yourself in your bedroom and listen to emo? I'm not judging unless you were wearing guyliner in which case we're in a fight. Write me back soon, because if you don't, then I have to do my homeworks and UGH.

Xo

Lacey

PS: Watch this one!

Jason clicked the link Lacey sent and saw that it was a video of the Mountain Goats covering the Jawbreaker song "Boxcar." He'd seen it before, which wasn't surprising. They were his favorite band, if you could call the Mountain Goats a band. It was sort of just one guy with a guitar, John Darnielle, though recently he'd been recording and touring with a bassist and a drummer. The music was both darker and less whiny than guys with acoustic guitars usually were, and Lacey loved it every bit as much as Jason did.

As the video played, he pictured Lacey watching it in her school's computer lab, imagining her mouthing the words and bobbing her head, squealing quietly with glee as soon as the song ended, while a disapproving teacher looked on.

He read the note again, savoring every word. These messages were like a window showing him a narrow sliver of Lacey's life. Sometimes he wanted to pry the window open with a crowbar and take in the entire picture. He'd never say it out loud for fear of sounding like a creepy stalker, but he wanted to know how she spent every waking moment — everything she said, who she sat next to in class, what she ate for lunch, the most-played songs on her iPod.

When he'd first messaged her, he'd known it was a long shot. It was her quote that caught his eye.

```
but none of the money we spend
seems to do us much good in the end
i got a cracked engine block, both of us do.
yeah, the house and the jewels, the Italian race car
they don't make us feel better about who we are.
i got termites in the framework - so do you.
```

It was the same one he had on his page, from one of his favorite Mountain Goats songs. They weren't the only two people on Facebook who listed it, but Lacey was definitely the prettiest. Something about her sleepy smile caught his eye. Her profile picture was a candid shot, not posed or stiff like the pictures of lots of girls Jason went to school with. Her eyes weren't fully open and she looked like she was about to burst into laughter. The moment was so genuine, Jason felt like he knew her instantly — and instantly wanted to know more. Brighton wasn't far from Oakdale. Plus, what did he have to lose? A pretty girl he didn't know might reject him, so what else was new?

It had taken three months for her to respond. By the time the message came, he almost deleted it because the name Lacey Gray meant nothing to him at first. But she had a face that was hard to forget, and images of it flooded into his head when he reread the notification e-mail. Yet when he clicked the link to her message, she was almost exactly as he remembered, looking simultaneously carefree and wise. What he wouldn't give to be the person who put that smile on her face.

Haha, sooo funny that we both have that quote. I love that song!!!!!! I saw the Mountain Goats play at Brighton Ballroom last year and I literally lost my voice from singing along. Totally worth it. One of the best nights of my life!! What other music do you like? I loooove tMG, and Bon Iver and the Decemberists, but I also really like dance music. Lately I can't stop listening to Robyn!
Anyway, thanks for messaging me. Tell me the music you're into and maybe I'll make you a mix ;)

Jason had never considered himself prone to good luck, but he wondered if he'd won the lottery. She was naming all the artists from his iTunes most-played list. And was she flirting with him? He didn't have a ton of firsthand experience in such matters, but after a decade of observing Rakesh's social successes, he was pretty sure that wink at the end was a good sign.

Lacey,
Thanks for your message. We have the exact same taste in music! Except I don't dance that much, but I have been known to sing some Robyn in the shower, haha.

This is kind of embarrassing, but I'm really into '80s teen movies right now. Love watching them on the big screen at art house theaters and thinking about what it would have been like to see them when they first came out, before they'd been copied a million times. Have you ever heard of the Rosewood Theater? It's near my friend Rakesh's house and we've been going to midnight movies there since we were in middle school. That was where I first saw Ferris Bueller's Day Off — even in 7th grade, Rakesh was just like Ferris. I guess that makes me Cameron, only my dad doesn't have a Ferrari.

He was about to tell her his dad didn't even live with him, but something Rakesh had once said rang like an alarm bell in his brain: "If you can't play hard to get, at least don't be a psycho about it." He was complaining about one of his many admirers, and at the time, Jason had just rolled his eyes, but as he began getting to know Lacey he had newfound sympathy for the thick-eyebrowed freshman he'd noticed following Rakesh from class to class.

They had continued like that since their first exchange, sending each other MP3s and playlists they found on indie rock Tumblrs. He recommended '80s movies for her to see — *Some Kind of Wonderful*, *Pump Up the Volume*, *Heathers* (which he couldn't believe she hadn't even heard of). She forced clubby remixes and YouTube videos on him. He had brought up the possibility of them meeting in person a few times — once by suggesting they get tickets to see Sleigh Bells in the city. He'd held his breath after sending, and hadn't thought of anything else until he got her reply. Lacey took a day longer than usual to answer, and when she did, she failed to mention anything about them meeting, but he was so relieved and heartened that she hadn't disappeared completely that the next week, when they were IMing, he wrote, "I hope you don't think I'm weird for saying this, but I really want to meet you." A minute went by, and then she answered, "me too" and then a moment later "ugh, so annoying, mom came in my room. Brb." She hadn't been right back, but she e-mailed the next day as usual. There was no mention of them meeting, so he'd listened to the voice telling him to slow down and held his tongue.

Jason watched the video she'd sent again. He was about to start formulating a response when he heard the front door open from downstairs. Mark was home. He slammed his laptop shut and grabbed his history book in case his mom came to his door to announce dinner was served.

When Jason finished washing the dishes that night, he returned to his room, shutting the door carefully behind him. Normally, there were clothes strewn about the floor and half the time his comforter could be found on the floor after he'd kicked it off in the night, but his mother had read him the riot act the previous weekend: Either he cleaned up his room himself, or she did, and there was no telling what she would throw away if she got her hands on it. And so he spent Sunday afternoon folding gray and white T-shirts and placing them in the wooden dresser that had belonged to his father when he was a kid. Jason alphabetized the records he'd bartered for at Vinyl Exchange and won in late-night eBay auctions and stacked them in crates he'd dragged in from the garage. He'd made the bed with new navy-blue sheets his mom had bought him, and once everything was in place, she had helped him hang concert flyers and vintage movie posters he'd collected on his bare white walls. All week, Jason had been admiring his handiwork. A hand-printed sign for a Wild Flag show he'd been to that summer adorned the wall above his bed, and Ferris Bueller, mischievous as always, gazed down at him as he did his homework. His mom had looked on silently as he'd hoisted the last frame, a color poster for *The Big Sleep*, one of his dad's favorite movies, onto the back of the door. Jason knew she didn't like to think of his dad if she could avoid it, but he was always grateful she never bad-mouthed him the way other divorced parents sometimes did. Instead, she'd told him he'd done a great job cleaning up, and then, before it turned into some sort of Hallmark moment, added, "Now you may return to your regularly scheduled destruction."

Settling into his desk chair, he logged in to Facebook. As he'd hoped, there was a green dot next to Lacey's name, and he forced himself to slowly count to ten before opening a chat with her.

Jason: Hey
Lacey: Hey yourself
Jason: You're not punk, and I'm telling everyone

It was the first line from the Jawbreaker song. He'd been planning to use the line since the second he'd opened the video.

He hoped she'd think it was clever, but now he worried she'd think it was mean. After a second, she answered with another quote from the song.

> **Lacey:** Seriously, how amazeballs was that?
> **Jason:** Pretty amazeballs.
> **Lacey:** Actually, all the videos the A.V. Club does are ridiculous. Titus Andronicus covering They Might Be Giants? Iron and Wine doing GEORGE MICHAEL? I MEAN.
> **Jason:** Haha
> **Lacey:** Can you even imagine how badass that room where they sign their names and the song they did must be? Gahh, I want to go to there.
> **Jason:** It's in Chicago I think. Have you ever been there?
> **Lacey:** This is so embarrassing, but when my brother was in middle school, he went to lacrosse camp there. And when we went to pick him up, I made my parents take me to the American Girl doll store.

Lacey had never mentioned a brother before. For the life of him, he could not remember a word Mr. Sharp had said about derivative functions in the last two months, but everything Lacey had ever told him was cataloged in his mind. She drove a standard-transmission Volkswagen that had once belonged to her grandfather, she hated chocolate, and she drank her coffee black. And she had a brother. For weeks, Jason had been meticulously drawing a mental picture of Lacey, and each time she fed him information he filled in new areas, as if bringing her to life. Each fact was like a new shade of paint studied closely before applying it to the canvas.

> **Jason:** I'm guessing this was last week?
> **Lacey:** Haha, exactly. No, I was 10, and I had a Molly doll I took with me EVERYWHERE.
> **Jason:** So your brother is older?
> **Lacey:** Yeah, 2 years older, but we're close. When he's not being a crazy jock frat boy in training. Do you have siblings?
> **Jason:** Nah, just me. It's how me and Rakesh got so close — we're both onlies and our parents used each other as babysitters. We watched a lot of Sesame Street together.

They went back and forth like that for the next half hour. Normally, when Jason was around girls, his brain went blank and his tongue tied up. When he imagined himself going on dates, he pictured himself opening doors and pulling out chairs and wowing with stories of his rock star heroics. But in real life when he tried to hold open doors for his classmates he felt like a security guard at the mall. As for the rock star thing . . . well, he had an 11:00 P.M. curfew on school nights. But with Lacey, everything was just as he imagined it should be. Yes, it was Facebook chat and not a hipster club in the city, but each conversation with her was like a date with his dream girlfriend. So why did he feel so weird about just asking her out?

> **Jason:** Sooo . . . I think I have to study for my history test.
> **Lacey:** Yeah, I should go too.
> **Jason:** But would you want to get together sometime? You know, IRL.

He felt like he'd see his heart pounding if he looked down, so he squeezed his eyes shut. He shouldn't have said "IRL," it was so cheesy. He shouldn't have said anything at all. Jason waited as long as he could before peeking at the screen.

> **Lacey:** Yes! Things are sort of . . . complicated right now. I'll explain more another time, but Jason, I do really want to meet you. You just have to give me a little time to figure out what's going on with me.
> **Jason:** Whenever you're ready. I just . . . like talking to you. ☺
> **Lacey:** ☺
> **Jason:** K, good luck with your homework.
> **Lacey:** Yeah, I'll try not to blow my brains out from boredom. Talk to you soon.

He breathed a deep sigh of relief. So what if it wasn't happening tomorrow? She wanted to meet him, and that was enough.

CHAPTER 3

W ho are you taking to formal, Jason?" Kelly Drummond asked, pulling Jason out of his reverie. "Rakesh seems to think getting a date will be no problem. So which lucky lady are you going to ask?"

Not for the first time, Jason wondered why he sat with Rakesh's friends at lunch. Some of them, like Lloyd Clifford, the star shortstop who Jason had met in Little League before he realized he sucked at baseball, weren't so bad. For the most part, though, their table was filled with kids who were so terrified of being different that they behaved like lemmings. Jason wasn't exactly shaving his hair into a Mohawk or painting his nails black, but the world outside Roosevelt High School seemed like a much more interesting place to blend into than the world inside of it.

"Don't worry about Jason," Rakesh answered. "Plenty of girls want to go with Jason."

"Oh, like who?"

Under other circumstances, Jason's feelings might have been hurt, but at the moment, he simply prayed Rakesh wouldn't say anything about Lacey. He could begin to imagine what Kelly would make of him liking a girl he only knew on Facebook, besides the fact that she'd probably tell everyone who would listen.

"Jason's got game you don't even know about."

"Speaking of game, are any of you watching the basketball team today?" Lloyd asked.

Relieved to be out of the spotlight, Jason shot one last nasty look at Kelly and went back to daydreaming about Lacey. He'd thought about asking her to the spring formal before. School dances hadn't held much appeal for Jason in the past. The music was all Top 40 and kids were more focused on snapping cell phone pics of one another than actually dancing. But you were supposed to ask a girl you liked to a dance, and Lacey would make a good date — they'd stand in a corner and spot the funniest outfits, the poufy dresses and ruffled tuxes that jocks wore ironically but that just made them look foolish. He'd request Robyn for her, and might even venture onto the dance floor.

On their way to history, Rakesh asked Jason whether he'd brought up the idea of the formal with Lacey.

"Not exactly," he answered begrudgingly.

"What are you waiting for? Kelly's only gonna get more annoying about it."

Jason knew he was right. Lacey said she needed time, and there was a month before the dance. Would that be enough?

"I don't want to rush her," Jason answered.

"Come on, you've been talking to her for weeks. I'm starting to think she's just stringing you along."

"Lacey doesn't play games." He said it as authoritatively as he could, but he couldn't help but think of how they'd ended their last conversation. *Things are sort of . . . complicated right now.* What did that even mean? As much for himself as for Rakesh, he quickly added, "Besides, it's a stupid dance. I don't even care whether or not I go."

Lowering himself into the dingy gray desk, Jason snuck a look at Facebook. Lacey had written him a long message. He skimmed it, and the tension in his chest eased as he read her jokes about her school's band and saw that she'd included a long pro and con list describing her feelings about Vampire Weekend. It was the same old Lacey. Sliding his phone back into his pocket, he wondered what he'd gotten so worked up about.

He took out his notebook and instinctively turned to the back, where he jotted down lyrics, but he caught Rakesh peering over from the desk next to his. He quickly turned to a fresh page and wrote the day's date in bold letters at the top. He willed himself to pay attention to the lecture, but there was a voice in his head drowning it out, one that sounded conspicuously like Kelly Drummond laughing at him. *Oh, like who?* Sometimes the idea of Lacey liking him seemed too good to be true. As his dad always said, when something seemed too good to be true, that's usually because it was.

CHAPTER 4

Jason liked any homework that required his computer. For one thing, if he had to use the Internet, he knew he'd be good at the assignment. For another, being online gave him an excuse to check Facebook. The history project was so easy he could spend five minutes on Google, and then use the next hour to chat with Lacey. If she wasn't online, he could at least compose a response to the Vampire Weekend pro and con list she'd sent him earlier.

Mrs. Kimball had warned her class not to rely on Google or Wikipedia, but Jason was convinced the forty-some-odd candles on her most recent birthday cake had blinded her to how useful they were. It's not as if Jason trusted everything he found online, but he knew enough to recognize the kind of primary source she'd asked them to find. As he predicted, finding a scanned letter from the nineteenth century was easy. He clicked print, and was about to turn his attention to Facebook when he had an idea.

He'd never Googled Lacey. Every piece of information he had about her, she had given him or he had gleaned from her status updates. As he typed her name into his search bar, he felt a twinge of guilt about cyberstalking her, although he wasn't expecting it to turn up much. He'd searched for his own name last year and found a veterinarian specializing in large animals;

a Hawaiian painter whose work looked like it was influenced by Woodstock flashbacks; and a private investigator who promised thoroughness, discretion, and sensitivity to the pain of a cheating spouse. Three quarters of the way down the second page of results was his postage stamp–size Facebook profile picture — one of the few photos of him that didn't make him look either deranged or like an overgrown eight-year-old.

He hit ENTER, and scanned the page until his eyes registered the by now familiar photo of Lacey from her Facebook page. He clicked the text automatically, but the moment the page loaded he realized he'd made some sort of mistake. The headline glared at him from the screen.

TEEN KILLED; BODY FOUND AFTER LOCAL PARTY

He blinked. On the monitor, Lacey's name blinked back at him. He rubbed his eyes. It was still there.

TEEN'S BODY DISCOVERED IN
BRIGHTON BACKYARD MONDAY

After Brighton High junior Lacey Gray was reported missing over the weekend, a body believed to be hers was found yesterday in the backyard of Steven and Grace Choi.

Lacey Gray, a budding musician and volunteer at the Hanson Place Soup Kitchen, was last seen at an unsupervised party at the Chois' house on Friday night. According to several sources, she did not return home after the party, and on Saturday morning friends and family began a frantic search for the honor roll student, who had never disappeared before.

Grace Choi, who was in Florida with her husband at the time of the party, discovered the body after returning on Monday morning, and immediately called the police. Despite numerous requests from the *Brighton Times*, the Brighton Police Department has neither confirmed that the body has been positively identified as Lacey Gray, nor the cause of death, but a memorial service for Gray has been scheduled for Saturday morning at the Brighton Unitarian Church on Johnson Avenue.

The Gray family has declined requests for interviews, and, through a lawyer, asked that their privacy be respected in this difficult time. Brighton High principal Lynn Darnell released the following statement: "Lacey Gray was a kind, vivacious young woman with a bright future, and her loss will be felt deeply by those who knew her and by the entire Brighton community." Darnell added that grief counseling will be available to all students.

In addition to her parents, Ed and Leslie, Gray is survived by her brother, Luke, a senior at Brighton High School, and cocaptain of the lacrosse team that took home the state championship last year. The family has asked that in lieu of flowers, donations be made to the Hanson Place Soup Kitchen.

His brain sprinted through the possible explanations: It was another Lacey Gray, it was another town called Brighton, it was all just a terribly unfortunate coincidence. The problem he couldn't get around was the photo. The photo he knew better than any photo of himself, better than any photo of anyone. It was Lacey's profile picture. Frozen, mid-laugh, the girl of his dreams was right there in front of him. Maybe he was hallucinating. He pinched himself — hard. It hurt, but none of the text in front of him changed.

I got termites in the framework — both of us do. The cheerfully desperate lyrics rang in his ears.

Jason felt dizzy and nauseated. He clicked the red *x* to close the on-screen window and stared at his computer. He tried to focus on the photo of the Mountain Goats playing live he'd saved as a desktop background, but everything went blurry. It had to be some sort of mistake. Or a joke. Rakesh was playing a prank on him. It wasn't a funny prank, but Rakesh had crossed the line before. He'd once witnessed Rakesh, with tears in his eyes, telling a girl from another school he had terminal cancer, and he wanted to spend some time with her before he died. When she'd figured out what was actually going on, she was so horrified that she'd never spoken to him again. He'd tried to send Jason to smooth things over with her, but as soon as she realized Jason had known Rakesh was healthy (if stupid) all along, she splashed a glass of water on his face.

Even though Rakesh would go to great lengths for a laugh, this seemed out of his scope. Everything else on the *Brighton Times* website looked completely legitimate. More than that, the details were too real. He hadn't told Rakesh — or anyone — that Lacey had a brother named Luke. And really, when you thought about it, *nothing* about this situation was funny.

He glowered down at his laptop accusingly. A very small part of him wanted to hurl it out the window, walk out of his room, and never think about Lacey again, but a bigger part of him needed to get to the bottom of this. He glanced over his shoulder to make sure his door was shut — the last thing he wanted was for his mother or, worse, Mark, to casually saunter in to drop off his laundry or inquire about the homework that was definitely not getting done — and reopened his browser.

The article was dated in October. Three and a half months before he and Lacey had begun talking. Right around the time he'd messaged her the first time. Slowly, nervously, he read the entire story again. His eyes scanned the words "body discovered" and "her loss will be felt deeply by those who knew her" and the sensation of a sharp dagger slicing through his entire world was replaced by a dull throbbing in his gut. It was an upgrade, he decided. Maybe the next phase would involve numbness kicking in.

He clicked back to his search results and opened the next story. This one was dated in January. He did some quick calculations in his head and figured it had been written shortly before he'd first heard from Lacey.

AFTER TRAGIC ACCIDENT,
TOWN STRUGGLES TO RECOVER

Three months after the sudden loss of a beloved teenager, her family and friends gathered together on a cold but bright morning in Brighton Park to celebrate her life. The school year, which started out promisingly for Lacey Gray, has been cast with a dark pall since October when Gray fell to her death during an unsupervised party hosted by a classmate. Her passing has been called a tragic accident, and Brighton High's class of 2014 has felt her absence deeply. "We didn't want to wait to dedicate a yearbook page to her," says Gray's friend and classmate Jenna Merrick. "We wanted her family to know we think about her and miss her every day."

Merrick led fundraising efforts to open the memorial in Brighton Park, and tears shone from her eyes yesterday as she stood next to the copper sculpture depicting a young girl dancing. Ed and Leslie Gray, Lacey's parents, and her brother, Luke, looked on, at times breaking down into tears, other times laughing as their daughter's friends took turns remembering Gray as a charismatic, promising young woman whose time on this earth ended entirely too soon.

Belinda Burns, longtime Brighton High English teacher, spoke of Gray's passion for poetry, and read verses from Rumi aloud to honor Lacey's memory. Those lines were engraved on a plaque that was unveiled beneath the sculpture. The plaque was a gift from the Palmer family, whose son Troy is a Brighton senior and one of Luke Gray's closest friends.

After attendees observed a moment of silence, they were invited to share their memories of Gray. "There wasn't a band she didn't know," recalled Max Anderson, a friend who had gotten to know Gray during their guitar lessons together. Anderson, who regularly performs in Brighton's smaller venues, played one of Gray's favorite Bright Eyes songs in her honor.

To close the ceremony, Ed Gray offered a few words. "This morning I would have traded anything in the world to spend even one more day with my daughter. But hearing what she meant to all of you, to this community . . . it makes me feel like her spirit is still with us. Thank you for keeping her alive."

Jason massaged his temples and shut his eyes. When he opened them again, he was surprised to find tears on his cheeks. He wasn't sure what, exactly, he was grieving. Wiping them away, he clicked through the photos that accompanied the story. In the first, the smiling Lacey he'd been falling for over the past several weeks gazed out of the screen at him. He took a moment and stared back, trying to figure out what she was trying to tell him, but her face remained forever stuck in that moment of joy, inscrutable as ever. The sculpture Lacey's friends had dedicated to her depicted a girl dancing, arms out to her sides, palms open, head tilted, a serene smile spread out across the copper face. In the third picture, a photograph showed Lacey as a young girl, twirling with a friend in a grassy field. It was clearly the moment the sculpture had been modeled on. "Lacey was as much a sister as a friend," Jenna Merrick (pictured at age 8, with Lacey, above) remembered. "I can't imagine what life looks like without her."

Me and J Money have been friends practically since we were born — we're family at this point.

Lacey had typed those words to him. Except maybe she hadn't.

The strangest part was that this was what he'd wanted to find. Not her obituary — that had never even crossed his mind. But evidence that the girl he'd been talking to was real. That she was as beautiful and smart and lovable as she seemed over IM. And she was all of those things. Everything she'd told him about the bands she loved, about learning to play guitar, about the New Age English teacher, all of that was exactly as he wanted it to be. It was like he'd been searching for a glass of water and instead found himself at the edge of an ocean armed only with his hands. As he tried to scoop out the water, it slipped through his fingers and a moment later he was up to his waist in it.

Half an hour before, he'd been sure Lacey was the solution to all of his problems; now he had no idea what to think. His head had filled with fog, and his body felt more tired than it ever had in his life. It was quickly becoming clear this wasn't a minor mix-up or a joke Rakesh was playing on him. But the truth seemed impossibly distant and dark. If it wasn't a prank, did that mean he was talking to a ghost? Or did it mean Lacey Gray was still alive?

CHAPTER 5

*M*oreland! You're slower than my grandmother, and she's in a wheelchair!" Coach Caroline Walker's PE class was tough even on the best of days. On this particular morning, exhausted from sleeplessness, Jason wondered if collapsing on the spot might provide some relief from the suicide drills she was forcing them to run.

When he'd said good night to his mom the night before, she'd taken his laptop to the living room — it was something she did casually, as if she were grabbing a load of his laundry or straightening up his schoolbooks, but he knew she did it to keep him from going online when he should have been sleeping. He'd considered sneaking downstairs to retrieve it, but he also wanted to forget every strange, confusing piece of information it contained about Lacey Gray. Maybe if he left it there, he reasoned, the news stories about her death and her friends would disappear. And so he'd spent the night kicking at his sheets and staring at the ceiling, trying unsuccessfully to separate the girl he knew from the girl in the obituary he'd read.

He wasn't sure what time he'd finally drifted off, but when his alarm sounded in the morning he jolted up from a dream where he'd been falling from the sky, plummeting toward an Earth that was nowhere in sight. For a moment, as he wiped the sleep from his eyes, he'd groggily thought the horrible news of the day before had been part of the same nightmare, but the very real memory of finding the *Brighton Times* article came flooding back in an icy rush. He'd hoped school would distract him from the questions he didn't even know how to begin to ask, but so far he'd had little luck.

PE was a class most kids slacked off in, but Coach Walker took the obesity epidemic very seriously, and, Jason thought, perhaps a little personally. She seemed determined to turn all of her students into Olympians, no matter how un–athletically inclined they were. This morning she wore a red and black Windbreaker and barked directions from beneath a yellowing basketball net.

"Three more sets to go! Slowing down isn't going to make this any easier, O'Donnell!"

The ancient gym was freezing. The air inside was damp, and it reeked of generations of sweaty teenagers. Jason had spent entire pickup basketball games and volleyball matches wondering whether kids in the '90s just didn't use deodorant. Smells like teen spirit indeed.

The whistle sounded and he reversed direction, gasping for breath as Meredith Singer, a stocky blonde who played trumpet in the school jazz band, blew past him. He pushed the mess of brown hair back from his forehead and did his best to keep up. The problem was that the faster his mind raced, the slower his legs wanted to go, and try as he might, he couldn't turn off his brain.

Snippets of conversations with Lacey floated through his head. *Things are sort of . . . complicated right now.* Complicated because you're dead? *You just have to give me a little time to figure out what's going on with me.* Well, yes, I imagine a dead person *does* have a lot to figure out.

If he hadn't been so distracted, he'd have enjoyed the sight of his gym-short-clad classmates all panting like Labradors, sliding to a stop and turning on their heels each time they heard the shriek of the whistle. On an average day, he would have daydreamed about swapping out prom portraits in the yearbook with ones from gym class, everyone sweaty and pink-cheeked and breathless. But this wasn't an average morning, and his normal disdain for his fellow students had morphed into envy at their Facebook feeds, which contained nothing more threatening than evidence of their latest breakups or unflattering photos from the sophomore camping trip.

He limped through the last of his sprints and then dragged himself into the dank locker room to change for history. The school had showers, but Jason had never seen anyone use them, and for all he knew water wouldn't even come out if you turned them on, but gym teachers were required to give their classes ten minutes to clean up — a rule Coach Walker followed only grudgingly.

Jason quickly pulled on a gray-and-white-striped T-shirt and narrow black corduroys, and drew his phone from his bag. He had nine minutes until history started. For a moment he just stared at the screen. What was he going to do — Facebook Lacey? He glanced over his shoulder and watched as Marcus Segal painstakingly folded his Roosevelt High basketball shorts and lined his sneakers up perfectly in his locker. Sometimes other people's problems were so obvious from the outside. If Marcus wasn't so anal about everything, people would like him more. He wished someone would sit Marcus down and explain it to him, but now wasn't the time. He'd told Rakesh he'd meet him in the quad before history. He checked his watch. If he hurried, he wouldn't be late, and it would leave him exactly five minutes to explain what had happened the night before. Jason had no idea where he would even start.

"Hey, man." Rakesh was leaning comfortably against the flagpole with mirrored Wayfarers on, the white frames popping brightly against his brown skin. "You ready to drop some crazy civil war knowledge?"

Jason had entirely forgotten about his homework. Briefly, he returned to his real world problems, and then he remembered he'd shoved the Robert E. Lee printout into his book bag before tumbling down the Lacey Gray Google rabbit hole.

"I'm just hoping she doesn't call on me," Jason said. "I have, like, two letters, and I barely even looked at them."

"Yo, even I did this one. What, were you busy last night?" Rakesh was skeptical. Online assignments weren't hard.

"Something, uh, sort of happened. . . ." Jason trailed off as they made their way into the main building and down the hall. Rakesh already rolled his eyes every time Lacey was mentioned. Was he going to think Jason was stupid — or worse, crazy — for getting tangled up with someone who was . . . Jason still wasn't sure what exactly Lacey was.

"What does 'something, uh, sort of happened' even mean?"

Jason looked around to see if anyone was listening. "You have to promise not to say anything."

"Dude, what's with the secrets all of a sudden? It's like one of us is James Bond, except that I'm not sure it's me, and I have a *serious* problem with that."

"Will you please just lower your voice?" Jason snapped, looking over his shoulder. "I don't want to talk about this here. Can we go to Michael's?"

"Leave school in the middle of the day?" Rakesh said with mock horror. Then he shrugged and grinned. "Sure, why not?" Rakesh kept smiling as they exited toward the parking lot. "But for the record, I am totally the James Bond of the two of us."

"So walk me through this again," Rakesh said ten minutes later as a waitress slid a plate overflowing with steak, eggs, potatoes, and pancakes in front of him.. Michael's was an all-night diner on the edge of town. It boasted an all-you-can-eat salad bar that consisted mostly of iceberg lettuce and ranch dressing, but the real draw was the roomy booths and the cheap menu that offered breakfast all day. It was where kids went after parties got broken up, and on nights when there were no parties but everyone was sick of the Wawa parking lot.

"While I was doing my history homework last night, I Googled her."

"You hadn't Googled her before?"

"I'm not some sort of stalker."

Rakesh scoffed.

"No, really, I'm not. I mean, I know you think I get a little carried away when I like someone —"

"Last year you read every post on Julia Granholm's wall dating back to eighth grade, and then you made me read them, too. Forget carried away — try obsessed."

"This is different," Jason continued. "And I'm not just saying that. The thing about Lacey is that, for once in my life, it felt like I might have a *real* girlfriend. Not someone I fantasized about marrying in the fifth grade like Nicole Trufardi. Not someone like Tanya Bellows, who sends me misspelled notes telling me I'm sweet and not someone I only liked because she looks like a swimsuit model, which I still maintain Julia Granholm does. With Lacey, I thought this is what it feels like getting to know someone you like and who likes you. This is what it's *supposed* to feel like. Until . . ."

"Until you found out she was dead," Rakesh said flatly, his mouth full of eggs.

"I still don't know if she *is* dead!"

"Okay, you found an obituary for a girl who looks and sounds like the girl you've been dating online who you've never met in person, and then you found another article that adds another nail to her coffin. Literally. Am I missing anything?"

"No, but . . ."

"So you're in love with a ghost? Is this what those Twilight books are about?"

"I'm not in love with anyone! Also, don't pretend you haven't seen all of the Twilight movies in the theater the weekend they came out."

"Would you say no to Katie Betz?"

"That doesn't explain why *New Moon* made you cry. And not the point! Can we go back to talking about me, please?"

"Sure, yeah, we can definitely go back to talking about how you're in love with a ghost."

Jason slumped against the booth. "I shouldn't have said anything."

"Look, as you know, I think it's a bad idea to date anyone you haven't met in real life, no matter how alive or dead she is. It's like I told you when you first started messaging 'her'" — he used air quotes around the pronoun — "for all you know, it's a dude at the other end of your messages. Or some lonely middle-aged whack job. But if you really like this girl, then I'm going to help you."

"Help me how?" Jason was always wary of the plans his friend dreamed up.

"Let me do a little digging tonight. There's something about this story that's weirdly familiar. Not to mention I want to see what the girl who's gotten your panties in such a twist looks like."

Jason would never have admitted it out loud, but a small part of him worried what would happen if Lacey met Rakesh. With his love of Top 40 radio and popped collars, he wasn't what he imagined Lacey going for, but he had yet to meet the girl who was immune to Rakesh's charm. "If I told you to forget it, would you let it go?"

"Not a chance. But I promise I won't steal her from you. Bro code, yo! I love you, man."

Jason rolled his eyes as he did whenever Rakesh began invoking the bro code or reciting silly, sentimental lines from buddy comedies. He wasn't happy to have been so transparent about his fears, but he was a little reassured.

"Fine," he sighed. "But you're buying this lunch. For my emotional hardship."

"You should be buying me lunch! I'm about to save you from yourself."

"Do you want to find another ride back to school?"

"I'll pay for your grilled cheese, but you owe me."

CHAPTER 6

When the final bell rang at the end of the day, Jason headed to the library. He'd wanted to start investigating Lacey as soon as possible, but Rakesh had squash practice — a sport his mom forced him to play. He pretended to hate it, but he was one of the best players in the state, and it was no secret Rakesh enjoyed the attention that came with his rank. Not to mention the fact that colleges were already contacting him about playing on their teams.

Jason studiously avoided the computers and instead settled himself at a desk tucked away behind the biography shelves where he cracked open his copy of *Hamlet*. The night of their first assignment, he'd sat in front of his computer, skimming the opening act with one eye while the other closely observed his Facebook chat list, waiting for Lacey to sign on. Ghost stories weren't his thing. At least, as of last week, they weren't. But this afternoon, with his scuffed-up New Balances propped on the extra chair he pulled up, he began to read in earnest. He went slowly at first, methodically untangling the thorny Shakespearean language, but as he began to get a feel for the characters, he sped up, not minding when he missed a word or two. Jason and Hamlet had more in common than he would have guessed — manipulative jerks for stepfathers, crushes on girls who probably shouldn't like them back, channels open with the friendly neighborhood ghost. He was fully absorbed in the drama of Denmark when he heard the faint buzzing of his phone in his bag. Fumbling for it, he saw that he'd missed three calls and two texts from Rakesh.

"Hello?" he whispered.

"Yo, you were right. She's totally hot!" Rakesh's voice blared through the speaker. "Where are you?"

"In the library. Wanna meet me at my car?"

"No, man, I got a ride home when I realized you had better things to do than answer my calls. Not cool, by the way. Come over. I have something to show you."

Tanya Adams answered the door at Rakesh's. She wore loose linen pants, a white tunic, and fuzzy shearling slippers. Her eyes lit up when she saw her visitor. "Jason, so nice to see your face, how are you?"

"I'm good, Mrs. Adams, how are you?"

"I can't complain." She kissed him on the cheek while welcoming him into the hallway. "Please, you must eat something. I made a casserole for dinner." Jason hadn't eaten since Michael's. He was torn between the urgency to find Rakesh and see what he'd discovered and the gnawing pains in his stomach. As if sensing his dilemma, Mrs. Adams added, "Come on, I'll make you a plate to eat with Rakesh, and in return you will tell him he must clean that nasty pit he calls his room."

"Okay, thank you, Mrs. Adams."

Jason enjoyed the aroma of spices as she piled broccoli next to the square of eggplant casserole on his plate. The Adams household was strictly vegetarian, and Rakesh's mother would flip if she knew about the sausage and bacon he devoured at

Michael's. Still, as much as Jason liked cheese fries and hot wings, he had a soft spot for the health food Mrs. Adams had been serving him since childhood. She asked about Jason's mom and Jason passed along her regards before he ventured upstairs. Bruno Mars was wafting down the hallway when Jason knocked on Rakesh's closed door.

"What!" he shouted angrily from within. Jason let himself in, and Rakesh laughed. "Oh, I thought you were my mom coming up here to tell me to clean my room."

"Oh yeah, she told me to tell you to clean your room."

"Whatever. We have important business to discuss."

A small part of Jason hoped all the stories he'd seen last night had disappeared when Rakesh tried to search for them. Sure, it would mean he was crazy, but on the other hand, he'd have a living, breathing girlfriend — or at least a shot with a living, breathing girl, which was more than he had now. He braced himself for what Rakesh had to say.

"This Lacey Gray situation is crazy." Jason sat down on Rakesh's bed, too nervous to respond. Rakesh continued speaking excitedly. "So, I remembered why her name seemed familiar. It's her brother, Luke. Remember last year during the Roosevelt-Brighton game? He had that illegal check on Aaron Sparks that dislocated his shoulder. It basically ended the season for the team."

Jason didn't follow Roosevelt High sports the way Rakesh did, but it sounded vaguely familiar. Aaron Sparks had been a big-shot senior, and even though Jason wasn't among those who compared his injury to crimes against humanity, it had been all anyone could talk about for a while. *Crazy jock frat boy in training.* That was how Lacey had described her brother. He wished he'd asked what she meant.

"That was him?" Jason said weakly.

"Yeah, and his buddy Troy Palmer is the class act who laughed about it from the sidelines. I hate those guys."

At least these details verified Lacey's existence. Lacey was a real person. She really had a brother and a life. It was what he'd wanted for so long, but it no longer felt like a gift.

"Anyway, I realized all this," Rakesh went on, "when I searched for Lacey on Facebook."

"Did you find her?" Jason asked. He wasn't sure he wanted to hear the answer.

"Yes, but . . ." For the first time, Rakesh's enthusiasm wavered.

"What?"

"I didn't exactly find her profile." He turned away from Jason and began fidgeting with the seal-shaped paperweight that sat on his desk. "I found a page dedicated to Lacey Gray. It's all messages written to her after she died."

So this was what Hamlet felt like when he saw the ghost, Jason thought. He was crazy. It was that simple.

Sitting at his computer, talking over his shoulder, Rakesh opened Facebook. "So I looked her up, right? And the people who show up — here's one in Oklahoma, here's one who goes to Cal State, and there's a bunch more, but none of them are from Brighton. But look, below that, there are pages. And here's the Lacey Gray memorial page."

He clicked it, and Jason left the bed to get a closer look.

He couldn't believe he'd never seen it before. It was a different photo. This one was posed, the type of thing that would go above your name in the yearbook. Her hair was more carefully styled, less rumpled, but the eyes were the same deep watery blue, the smile that even now flopped Jason's stomach. It was so obviously the same girl.

> **Lacey Michelle Gray**
> **August 18, 1996–October 5, 2012**
> Your grief for what you've lost lifts a mirror
> Up to where you're bravely working
>
> Expecting the worst, you look and instead,
> Here's the joyful face you've been wanting to see.
> — Rumi

Rakesh stayed mercifully silent as Jason took it in. The birthday, the date of her death, the poetry. The joyful face he'd been wanting to see. Set against the blue and white background where he was so used to seeing her, this was somehow worse than the obituary. This felt like a betrayal. He read the testimonials her friends had written.

> Luv u lacey. Miss u 4ever

> Lacey, we sat next to each other in English all year, and I never got a chance to tell you how special I think you are. Even though lots of people at this school make me feel like I'm invisible, you always made me feel like you really cared about me every time we talked. When you found me crying in the bathroom after my cat died, you didn't make fun of

me or tell anyone how stupid I looked with all that mascara on my cheeks. Instead you skipped English so I wouldn't have to be alone. I will remember you forever.

LACEY I HAD THE BEST TIME WITH YOU AT THE 8TH GRADE SPRING DANCE. I WILL NEVER DANCE TO "I KISSED A GIRL" WITHOUT THINKING ABOUT YOU. LOVE YOU ALWAYS

Lace face, I'm so sorry you're gone. I miss you every day, but I know you're up there somewhere looking down on us.

I still can't believe you're gone and I never got to tell u how I really feel. Some days I feel like the sun will never shine again without you here to see it.

The queasiness in his gut increased with each new message. He scrolled down for what seemed like forever, reading until he couldn't take it anymore, and then walked wordlessly back to the bed and sat down with his hands on his knees.

Jason didn't know how long they sat like that before Rakesh finally asked, "What do you think it means?"

"It means someone named Lacey Gray is dead." His voice sounded odd, like he was being strangled while he spoke.

"Okay," Rakesh drew out the word, choosing his next ones carefully. "J, the girl you've been talking to, is it this girl?"

"I know you think I'm crazy," Jason began, but Rakesh cut him off.

"That's her picture, that's her high school, blah blah blah. But is this the girl you've been talking to? Her profile, I mean?"

Jason was having a hard time following what Rakesh was saying. "No, that's not it."

"Why can you see her profile but I can't?" Jason looked at him blankly. When he didn't answer, Rakesh added, "I *don't* think you're crazy. But something crazy is definitely going on here. I want to know what."

Amid all the confusion in his mind, Jason felt a rush of gratitude for his friend. He thought of Horatio and Marcellus swearing the oath on Hamlet's sword. "Hold on, let me try something." He gestured for Rakesh to get up.

Sitting down at the computer, he logged out of Rakesh's Facebook account and in to his own. He noticed Rakesh had changed his profile picture to a James Bond portrait. Jason asked him about it.

"I had Bond on the brain," he said with a smile.

Jason began typing in the search bar at the top of the page. He'd entered L-A-C when two recommendations dropped down. The first was the profile picture he was so familiar with. The second was the page he and Rakesh had just examined. He couldn't believe he'd never seen it before. With the mouse, he hovered over the first one and looked at Rakesh.

"Go on!" he said impatiently, and Jason clicked.

As he did so, he tried to envision what her profile had looked like the last time he'd checked it. He'd noticed early on that it was restricted — she could post status updates but no one else could post on her wall. It wasn't exactly conventional to hide your wall like that, but Jason had chalked it up to her renegade spirit; the generic girls who treated high school like a beauty pageant could have all the inside jokes and duck-face photos they wanted, but Lacey was keeping it simple and classy. He'd kept tabs on her silly statuses and shared links via his news feed, but he hadn't spent a lot of time on her profile.

He had the sinking feeling he'd missed something huge by not paying more attention, and as her profile loaded his fears were confirmed. Her wall at first seemed innocuous enough, littered with the updates that had inserted little jolts of joy into his news feed, but it was something on the left side of the page beneath the picture that now made him sick to his stomach:

Friends (1)
Jason Moreland

"Oh, *snap*," Rakesh breathed.

The status updates were for his eyes only. Rakesh was right, something crazy was going on. The boys exchanged a look, and Jason slowly backed away from the computer as if it were capable of attacking him.

"I guess the good news is that now we know you're the only guy in Lacey's life?"

Jason attempted to laugh, but the noise sounded strange and hollow. He really *had* wanted to be the only guy in Lacey's life. Through his daze, he heard Rakesh asking him what he was going to do now.

"I'm going to confront her." The response was as surprising to him as it seemed to be to Rakesh. But after the words were out of his mouth, he knew it was the only option.

"What are you going to say?"

Jason shook his head. "That is a good question. I'll let you know when I figure out the answer."

That night, in bed, he toggled back and forth between his messages and the memorial page. Seven hundred forty-six people liked it. In the past he had found himself ranting over the limits of the LIKE button. "Like" had no place when it came to a memorial dedicated to a sixteen-year-old girl who died. But that was the least of his problems right now. Seven hundred forty-six people wanted Lacey Gray to rest in peace. But Lacey Gray also had one friend no one knew about.

CHAPTER 7

Jason agonized over what to write to Lacey, but in the end she made it easy for him. Well, not exactly easy. His dreams that night were haunted by visions of himself trying and failing to compose messages to her. In one, he found himself at a typewriter equipped with keys too heavy to use. He pushed on them with all his might, but couldn't get a single letter to stick to the blank page. He was frantically searching for ink for a quill when his alarm roused him in the morning.

Still half asleep, he sat down at his computer and after he'd fumbled for his glasses, noticed the green dot next to Lacey's name. Without thinking, he typed, "I need to talk to you. It's important." It was so simple. He yawned and by the time he reopened his eyes, she'd replied.

> **Lacey:** I swear I'm not blowing you off.
> **Lacey:** Good morning, BTW.

Despite himself, Jason grinned.

> **Jason:** Good morning yourself.
> **Lacey:** Seriously, though, I have a test and I'm going to be late for school.
> **Jason:** Can we talk later?

Lacey: J, don't hate me, but this is a really bad time. Ughhhh, I'm so sorry, there's something going on with me right now. I need a couple days to myself. I promise, I will hear you out and explain everything after this weekend. Can you just trust me that long?

Jason: Yeah, of course.

Lacey: There's one more thing. A favor. I hate to ask.

Jason: . . .

Lacey: Can you not tell anyone we're talking?

Lacey: IT'S NOT YOU. I swear. And I know it sounds weird since it's not like you go to Brighton, but just until Monday.

Jason blinked. Why didn't she want anyone to know they were talking? Mark was shouting at him from downstairs to make sure he was awake. He yelled back that he was on his way.

Jason: My friends already know.

Lacey: Rakesh?

Jason: Yeah.

Lacey: I figured. Can you not tell anyone else? I'm not trying to be shady, but I really gtg. Monday, I swear. Do you trust me?

For someone who was clearly harboring a huge secret, Lacey was awfully big on trust.

Jason: Yeah.
Lacey: You are a lifesaver.

It was these last cryptic words he played over and over to himself later. *You are a lifesaver.* Lacey trusted him. He chose to focus on that when he recounted the exchange to Rakesh at lunch, though he purposefully left out the part where she had requested he not tell anyone, instead asking of his own accord.

"Can you not tell people about all this? I don't want anyone to think I'm crazy."

"Good luck with that. I have better things to talk about with my other friends than your weird zombie love story."

Jason doubted that were true, but he knew he could trust Rakesh to keep quiet about Lacey, at least for a couple days. A couple days was all he needed. *Monday, I swear.* It was a simple misunderstanding, and she was going to explain everything. He just had to trust her.

His heart sank when he walked into his house on Friday afternoon. He could sense it the second he came through the door, the dwindling light at his back. Boredom was waiting for him. Boredom had occupied every room, and beyond each room the entire town. It was inescapable. His mom and Mark were out to dinner in the city, not that he was unhappy they were gone. He flopped down in the den and flipped through all 450 cable channels. Nothing. His Netflix queue was filled with experimental documentaries and pretentious German movies he'd added in the hopes that he would someday be the type of guy who would enjoy experimental documentaries and pretentious German movies, but someday wasn't yet.

Retreating to his room, he turned on his computer. He'd vowed to steer clear of the Internet until he heard from Lacey, so instead of logging on to Facebook, he did what he'd done so many nights before, when the name Lacey Gray meant nothing to him. He scrolled through iTunes. For about the zillionth time, he settled on *All Hail West Texas*. He knew you were supposed to listen to it on tape, and he even had the cassette, but alas, he had no working tape deck, so digital would have to do.

Lying back on his carpet staring up at the ceiling, he moved his lips silently along with "The Best Ever Death Metal Band in Denton." And at first it worked. He got lost in John Darnielle's raw voice, belting out the lyrics like they were the only thing that mattered to him in the world. For the moment, they were. But when he got to "The Mess Inside" and all that talk of fighting the "sense of creeping dread with temporal things," it was like the spell was broken. He turned up the volume to see if he could drown out the voice in the back of his mind telling him he was fooling himself, but it was hopeless.

He was alone on a Friday night, and the one person who made him feel happy and whole was no longer making him feel happy or whole. He couldn't suddenly revert to the person he'd been before they'd begun talking, a person who had accepted those empty spaces as a fact of life, who thought happiness was overrated. And he wasn't going to last until Monday pretending that she didn't exist. The next thing he knew, he was in the kitchen, dragging the stepstool across the cool tile floor of the kitchen, climbing up, swinging open the cabinet above the fridge. Just as he remembered, next to the flashlights and bottled water his mom stored in case of emergency was a dusty copy of the Brighton County phone book.

When he was little, he'd seen his parents use it all the time, calling a shoe store to find out their hours or copying down the address of his doctor's office as they rushed out the door to an appointment. These seemed like ancient practices to him now. If he was visiting a store that didn't have a website, he looked it up on Yelp. But Jason had imposed the Internet ban on himself because he knew searching for the Gray family online would mean endless stories about Lacey's death and pages dedicated to her memory. So here he was flipping through the pages until he got to one that started with Graves and ended with Harris. His eyes followed his finger down the page until he reached the second listing for a Gray.

Gray, Edward . . . 3492 Belmont Rd. 621-9067

Jason's heart was pounding as he dialed. He wanted it to be disconnected, to ring through forever. It rang three times before a male voice picked up.

"Hello?"

Jason hung up immediately. It seemed silly — or more *insane* than anything else. What was he hoping would happen? That she'd answer the phone? And he'd ask her out? The idea was laughable. His hands were shaking when he looked down at them. He couldn't be alone for another minute. He silently pleaded Rakesh was not in a crowded car with LMFAO turned up too loud to hear his phone, but there was barely any noise in the background when he answered.

"Talk to me."

"What am I doing?"

"Um, playing board games with Blake Lively?"

"I'm being serious."

"Yeah, I knew Blake Lively would never talk to you."

"Rakesh."

"What do you want me to say, man?"

There was that question again. What did Jason want?

"I just called her house. Lacey's house."

"You *what*? What did you say?"

"I hung up."

"Of course you did. Wuss."

"What was I supposed to do?"

"Tell them their daughter's not dead. Even though she's probably dead."

"She's *not* dead." Jason surprised himself with the hard edge in his voice.

"Dude, do you really even believe that?"

He didn't answer. Belief was beside the point, he needed Lacey to be alive.

"Do you want me to come over?" Rakesh adopted a baby voice. "Do you want Daddy to make it better? I can rock you back and forth until you forget all about your lady trouble."

"Screw you."

"Hey, you called me."

Jason knew he was right, but he still refused to answer.

"Well, can I at least come over and play Xbox? My dad is watching some documentary about Nazis on the History Channel, and my mom is driving me crazy."

"Fine," he said sullenly. Another person in the house was better than the alternative, which was moving on to the really dark Mountain Goats songs. "How long will it take you to bike here?"

"How soon can you pick me up?"

They played video games long past midnight, and then Rakesh passed out on the sofa in the den, and Jason went up to his room and got in bed. Exhausted, he slept soundly, no haunting nightmares involving writer's block and bad wardrobe choices. When he woke late in the morning, he came downstairs in his sweats to find Rakesh cracking his mom up as she cracked eggs into a bowl. Jason rubbed his eyes.

"Hi, pookie," she said when she saw him, "I'm making Rakesh pancakes. Do you want any?"

"I can't even remember the last time you made me pancakes," he grumbled.

"You know that's because I'm her favorite son," Rakesh said, beaming at Mrs. Moreland.

She laughed. "It's true, Rocky, you are." No one had called him Rocky since elementary school, and he wouldn't answer when his own mother used it, but he tolerated it from Jason's.

Jason turned to Rakesh. "You're awfully chipper this morning."

"Dude, your mom's making me pancakes. My mom barely even buys enough Cheerios to get me through the week."

Jason plopped down at the kitchen table while rolling his eyes. "Yeah, it's a regular famine over at the Adams household."

"Hey, poor starving Oliver Twist," his mom chimed in, "blueberries or chocolate chips?"

"Chocolate chips," the boys said in unison.

She shook her head. "Why does that not surprise me?"

Jason relaxed as they ate breakfast. His mom asked about their teachers and then entertained them with stories of gross things she'd seen at the hospital. Jason couldn't count the number of times he'd sat at this table with Rakesh and his mom chatting easily while eating eggs or pancakes. It felt good to be normal.

After Rakesh left, he carried their dishes to the sink and began washing up. He felt better than he had the night before. It was going to be a good Saturday. Mark would be at the driving range until nightfall. He'd call his dad when his mom left for her yoga class, and then he'd catch up on his homework. He hadn't read Pitchfork all week — he could see if there was any new music worth caring about, and he could even drive to the city and buy it on vinyl if he felt energetic. He was going to keep boredom at bay.

"Honey, did you take this out?"

He cast a glance over his shoulder to see his mom holding the phone book. He could practically hear the record-scratching sound effect as the questions surrounding Lacey flooded back into his mind.

"Oh, um, yeah. I needed it . . . to order pizza last night. The number on Little Johnny's website is wrong." Lying was definitely simpler than explaining the situation to his mother, but he still felt a pang of guilt as soon as the words were out of his mouth.

"Do you still need it?"

"No, you can put it away," he answered. He said a quick prayer of gratitude that neither the fact that he ordered from Johnny's often enough to know the number by heart nor the lack of pizza boxes in the kitchen had tipped her off to his dishonesty. He heard her replace it above the fridge, and then she patted him affectionately on the shoulder before heading to her class.

Jason knew he wasn't going to keep Lacey out of his head today. He thought about calling the Grays again, but he was still unsure about what he could say, or what a conversation with them would accomplish other than give Lacey doubts about whether she could trust him. Still, he was going to lose his mind if he didn't do something. He grabbed his car keys from his room. He had an idea.

CHAPTER 8

There was a cold snap in the air despite the brightly shining sun. Jason hadn't worn a scarf, so he zipped his jacket as high as it would go and shoved his hands in the pockets when he got out of his car at Brighton Park. He used to come to the park with his father when he was younger. It had a wide grassy field that was perfect for setting off the model rockets they built together. They'd leave the house early, and it always felt like an adventure, though in retrospect Jason wondered if his dad was just avoiding his mom. He kept moving. On the average summer day, Jason knew, the ball field would be filled with sounds of children playing and bats cracking, but today, maybe because of the March chill, the park was deserted.

He made his way past the empty baseball diamond and through the well-manicured rocket-launching lawn. He saw a woman tossing a ball to her golden retriever, and two middle-aged men getting a morning workout in, but by the time Jason found the tucked-away semicircle of benches he'd been searching for, he was completely alone. There, in the open space the benches were facing, was the Lacey Gray memorial.

It was only as he approached it that he realized, too late, why he'd really come. He'd wanted to find nothing. A pit in the ground or Hollywood sign–size letters indicating this was a site dedicated to someone else, someone whose name was not Lacey

Gray. But this was definitely the memorial he'd read about in the *Brighton Times*.

The copper sculpture was smaller than it looked in the photograph, but shinier, too. Even from beneath the shade of a Japanese maple it was glinting with sunlight. Hesitantly, Jason advanced, his eyes never leaving the dancing girl. Even in sculptural form, Lacey was captivating. He knelt over to read the plaque at its base.

YOUR GRIEF FOR WHAT YOU'VE LOST LIFTS A MIRROR
UP TO WHERE YOU'RE BRAVELY WORKING

EXPECTING THE WORST, YOU LOOK AND INSTEAD,
HERE'S THE JOYFUL FACE YOU'VE BEEN WANTING TO SEE.
— RUMI

IN LOVING MEMORY OF LACEY GRAY, DAUGHTER, SISTER, FRIEND.
AUGUST 18, 1996–OCTOBER 5, 2012

Jason lowered himself onto the cold, hard earth, pulling his knees to his chest. There were flowers laid carefully on the ground around the sculpture, and stuffed animals, some bearing notes. If it had been someone else, Jason would have been overwhelmed with the injustice of it. A girl named Anya in his grade school had passed away from leukemia. He'd been too young to comprehend the loss, but at odd moments she'd come back to him, and he'd realize how strange, how sad, how utterly unfair it was that she never lived her life past the third grade.

But this was different. Lacey had IM'd him yesterday.

I have a test and I'm going to be late for school.

Anya didn't have tests; she didn't go to school. Anya had never even been on Facebook. Anya wasn't alive. Lacey was. She had to be.

Things are sort of . . . complicated right now.

Complicated didn't even begin to describe it.

Once again, he ran through the possibilities.

1. Lacey was communicating with him from beyond the grave. There were a lot of problems with this theory, not the least of which was that Jason was pretty sure he didn't believe in ghosts. But say Lacey was dead — why would her spirit have chosen Jason, a person she never knew, to contact? Sure, he had reached out to her first, but judging from the gifts left for her at the memorial, Lacey was not a person who was lacking for friends.

2. Someone was pretending to be Lacey. Compared to this option, Jason almost wished he had a ghost on his hands. Only someone cruel would impersonate a dead teenager, and whoever Jason was dealing with wasn't cruel. And again, he had to ask, why him? Jason may not have had a boatload of friends, but he certainly didn't have any enemies, and someone would have to want to hurt him to do this.

3. Lacey was still alive. A little thrill ran through his body when Jason considered this one. It wasn't just that he wanted it to be true — which he deeply, truly did — more that it seemed like the only real option. And yet it still didn't answer why she would allow her family and friends to believe she was gone. The Lacey he knew wouldn't hurt people around her like that.

When he had read and reread their messages and conversations, a theory had begun to form, and something about being here, in this space dedicated to her, helped it crystallize: She had sought him out because she had known they would have a real connection. Jason knew if he said it out loud, Rakesh would laugh in his face, but it added up. He had recognized something deeper in her when he found the Mountain Goats quote on her Facebook page, and she had seen a kindred spirit in him. But she had to be sure she could trust him before she revealed her secret — whatever it was. Jason just had to prove that he was committed to her, no matter what she was hiding.

"Did you know her?" The voice was soft and sweet, but Jason started when he heard it. He swiveled around and found a petite, fair-skinned girl standing over him. He stood, clumsily brushing the leaves and grass from his pants as he turned to face her. He tried to place her, but her face gave nothing away.

"Did I know her?" he finally squeaked when it registered that she'd been speaking to him.

The girl gestured to the sculpture. "Lacey. We built this for her. She passed away last year." She was clutching a bouquet of daisies in one hand as she spoke.

"Oh, um, no, I never met her." At least it wasn't a lie. Before she could ask what he was doing there, he hastily added, "I'm so sorry. Was she your friend?"

"My best friend," the girl said a little sadly.

And then he remembered Lacey's messages. *Me and J Money have been friends practically since we were born — we're family at this point.* So that was why she seemed so familiar. Her full name had been in the *Brighton Times* — it was Jenny. Or Jenna. He couldn't quite recall.

She leaned down to replace the wilting flowers at the memorial's base with the ones she'd brought. Jason took the opportunity to survey her more closely. She had dark hair that swung around her chin, and her pale skin and light eyes almost seemed to glow in contrast. The features on her face were small and delicate, and though she smiled at him as she straightened up, she had an air of mourning about her. "We wanted to make this the type of place that she'd want to visit."

"It's really nice," Jason said. "I mean, the sculpture. It caught my eye from the bike path. That's how I wound up here."

"It's funny. I think if she were around to see it, she *would* like it, and that makes it easier for me when I come here to talk to her." She cast a sidelong glance in his direction. "I hope that doesn't seem weird, you know, that I talk to her."

Not even close, he thought to himself. "I don't think it's weird." For a moment they stood side by side, observing the sculpture. She was only wearing a thin jacket, and she crossed her arms over her chest to keep herself warm. Jason thought about offering his own coat, but decided it would be weird. Finally, he broke the silence. "You must miss her."

"All the time. But when I come here, it's different. It's almost like she's not gone. I don't know. I don't talk to her because I think she can hear me, but sometimes it does feel like she's listening." As she spoke, she neatened up the tributes people had deposited there, lining up the stuffed animals, and brushing away dead leaves and twigs. She straightened up and studied Jason carefully — for a split second, he felt like she could see through him and knew exactly why he was there, but he realized he was being paranoid. "You must think I'm crazy," she said with a wry laugh. "Sometimes I have no filter."

"I don't think you're crazy," Jason said sincerely. "I can't even imagine what it's like to lose your best friend."

She smiled gratefully, before offering her hand to him. "I'm Jenna," she said. Arm outstretched, the resemblance to the child in the photo with Lacey was almost eerie.

"I'm Jason. It's nice to meet you. I hope you don't mind my being here."

"No, I mean, we wanted to put the memorial in a public park because Lacey liked being around other people so much."

It was as if Jenna knew one Lacey, the social butterfly, and he knew her shadow, who only had eyes for him. He was unsettled by it, as if one of them would slip away at any moment. He wanted desperately for his Lacey to come to life, but seeing the pained expression on Jenna's face made him feel selfish about not caring more about the one she had lost.

As shaken as he was by the duality, there was something about Jenna that put him at ease. When she spoke, the questions stopped swirling. Standing shoulder-to-shoulder with someone who knew the flesh-and-blood Lacey made him feel connected to the person beyond the avatar. He almost felt like he could trust Jenna. For the briefest of seconds, Jason was compelled to tell her Lacey wasn't a stranger, that, in fact, he knew her well. And then he remembered Lacey's warning. *A favor. I hate to ask. Can you not tell anyone we're talking?* Maybe this was all a test. Maybe she had known he'd come here.

"I think I, um, read something about her. About Lacey." He wanted to keep the conversation going, but he wasn't sure how. "Like, maybe on Facebook or something?"

Jenna studied him. "Are you from Brighton?"

"No, Oakdale."

"I don't know about in Oakdale, but around here it's pretty big news when a sixteen-year-old falls off a balcony during a party."

He winced at the harsh image. "I'm sorry, I didn't realize that's how she . . ." He trailed off. For some reason the word "died" wouldn't come out. He cleared his throat. "I didn't realize that's what happened."

"I didn't mean to get so intense about it, it's just . . . Facebook. It's really weird after you lose someone, you know? Like, everyone's posting random stuff about this thing that's really personal and deep, and they're all 'LOL' or they're talking trash. It's bizarre, like, Lacey's gone, and Facebook keeps happening." Jason couldn't make himself look at her as she spoke. *If you only knew* . . . he thought silently.

"I'm so sorry," Jason said. Why did he keep apologizing? "Did I already say that?"

"You did. But thank you."

He wanted to ask her more about Lacey, about what she was like in person and what kind of gossip people spread about her on Facebook, but he didn't want to agitate her, so instead he turned to leave. "Well, I should go," he said awkwardly. "I'll let you talk to your friend."

She pushed her hair back behind her ears. "It was nice to meet you, Jason. Sorry that got kind of weird. I get emotional sometimes."

"It's understandable. I'm sorry again. I'll stop saying that."

She laughed, and he smiled back. "Well, see you around." He wondered if he should ask for her e-mail or something, but he remembered he was just supposed to be passing through the park. He waved awkwardly, and made his way back along the path.

* * *

When he got to the parking lot, he was sweating, even though it was still chilly out. He sat in his car for a few minutes without starting it. His beat-up blue Subaru had been joined by a gleaming black Mercedes, a beat-up Volkswagen, and a crimson Toyota. All of them were empty, but his guess was the Camry was Jenna's. What had just happened with her? Jenna's approach, her rushed outpouring of emotion about Lacey, it was all so strange and sudden. He'd come here searching for some kind of clue that Lacey was alive, and instead he'd found the person who was supposed to be closest to her in the world talking frankly about how she wasn't.

When he put the key in the ignition he was overcome by the sensation that there was someone — or something — there with him. He scanned the rearview mirror, checking for company, and though he saw no one, his neck continued to prickle ominously. Leaning his head against the steering wheel, he whispered, "What's the story, Lacey? What am I missing?" He closed his eyes and tried to concentrate, but there was only silence.

CHAPTER 9

*J*ason took the long way home so he could listen to the entirety of *For Emma, Forever Ago*. It seemed somehow appropriate — he knew Lacey liked Bon Iver, and it was the only thing he wanted to hear anyway. He turned the volume up as high as it would go, and when he pulled into his driveway and removed the key from the ignition an hour later, the peace was borderline eerie.

Grabbing his phone from the cup holder, he saw he had a new message. It was from Rakesh.

Bonfire at the bridge tonight. Can you drive?

Some nights he'd have said no, either to avoid playing chauffeur or because he didn't feel like making small talk with people who looked right through him in the halls at school. But right now he'd give anything to get his mind off of Lacey.

Yeah, what time do you want me to pick you up?

Come at 7:30 — we can go to Michael's before.

But when he got to his room, he sat very still on his bed and stared at his phone. Ever since he'd left Jenna, he'd been fighting the urge to call Lacey's family again. It was like a scab he knew he shouldn't pick at but he couldn't help himself. He was finally starting to understand why pretty girls always went into the basement in horror movies, even when they had plenty of evidence that a masked murderer was lying in wait for them the second they got down the stairs. It felt a lot better than hiding under a bed. If he called Lacey's parents, they were going to tell him she was gone, just like Jenna had, but there was something thrilling about your worst fears, and something powerful about ignoring them.

He scrolled through his recent contacts and put through the call to her house.

He got it out in one breath. "Hi. May I speak to Lacey?"

The voice on the other end was ragged when it finally answered. "Who is this?"

"My name is Keith McKeller." It was the name of an aging hippie his aunt had dated briefly, and the first alias that popped into his head.

There was a sharp intake of breath, and then a weary exhalation. He could practically feel her father's grief as he answered, "Keith, I don't know who you are or how you knew my daughter, but she died last October."

There was a click as the line went dead. Jason called back more determined than he had been before. This time the "Hello?" had an edge.

"Sir, I'm so sorry to hear about your loss. I don't mean to bother you, but I'm the director of the, um, Orange County Guitar School, and we received an audition video from Lacey." Jason felt sweat beading at his temple. Mr. Gray was going to see through his lies.

"You're mistaken," said Mr. Gray firmly.

"It was sent to us three weeks ago, sir."

"That's not possible." There was no mistaking Mr. Gray's anger now. "There must have been some kind of mix-up."

"The video we have is from someone named Lacey Gray. She listed this as her home phone number. I was calling to tell her we'd love to accept her into our program."

"Are you listening to me? My daughter is gone. Whoever you are, leave my family alone. Please don't ever call here again."

Jason's hands were shaking when Ed Gray hung up the phone. It was like he'd been possessed during the call. During his yard work earlier, he'd been rehearsing what he might say, but he did that all the time — rarely did he follow through on the scripts. And maybe there was good reason for that. The conversation hadn't exactly been a rousing success. In retrospect he realized how foolish he'd been. There wasn't a chance he was going to hear what he wanted. *Why yes, complete stranger, my daughter* is *alive, but shhhh, don't tell anyone. Also, she would like to marry you.* No, instead of that totally realistic and not at all crazy response, he'd been confronted with Lacey's dad's raw grief, and now he felt like a terrible person. He felt something else, too. Anger at Lacey. Why was she doing this? And why was she keeping him in the dark? He would help her, but she would have to tell him how.

Parties didn't happen at the bridge so much as they happened under it, on a dark cement landing about the size of a grade-school playground. The underbelly of the bridge was decorated with colorful graffiti that had been there at least since the current Roosevelt High seniors were freshmen.

The first time they'd come to the bridge their sophomore year, Jason had been awed by the upperclassmen gripping red cups and dancing to music blasted from cordless iPod speakers.

This was the high school of John Hughes movies, not just the sleepy continuation of his middle school existence. But he quickly realized that bridge parties usually ended with shouts from park rangers or local police to break it up, causing all the kids to scatter to their cars before regrouping in the Wawa parking lot or at Michael's. Half the nights there was a squad car parked by the side of the road where you were supposed to hop the guardrail and trek down a steep wooded path to the flat concrete below. Jason was always secretly a little pleased on those nights — he didn't have to risk his limbs to spend his evening fearing the cops' arrival and they could go straight to the next location, where kids weren't constantly encouraging one another to turn the music down and you could actually see the person who was talking to you.

But tonight everything had gone according to plan, at least so far. The entrance to the bushwhacked path was open, and the cowboy boot–shaped flashlight on Jason's key chain had guided them down safely. He and Rakesh and Lloyd had done a lap, scouting the different groups clustered about. Rakesh and Lloyd were in the middle of debating which members of the girls varsity basketball team they would choose to rescue them from a fire, when a group of non-basketball-playing girls standing to their right captured Rakesh's attention. "Ladies!" he boomed, slinging his arms over two of their shoulders. "How goes it?"

Lloyd caught Jason's attention and rolled his eyes and then headed out to find a tree where he could relieve himself, and Jason turned to Gabe Wyffels. Hip-hop blared as he described his plans to become a competitive surfer after high school.

"People think surfing is just, like, this thing that burnouts in

Hawaii and Australia do, but it's an art, man. I mean, naw, it's not an art, it's a *sport*. It's a sport for *warriors*."

Jason stifled a laugh. He had watched the surfing videos Gabe had posted on Facebook, and there was no denying he could ride a wave, but he was far too easygoing to be called a warrior.

"So, do they, like, have scholarships for surfing?"

"I dunno. Sometimes I don't really think college is for me. It's just, like, this *plan* that they have for us, you know? But I don't wanna live someone else's plan. I'll chart my *own* destiny. Oh, hey, did you just hear that?"

Jason looked around. He hadn't heard anything, but everyone around them froze, murmuring to one another about the noises. The vigilance wasn't doing much to soothe Jason's jangled nerves. He couldn't stop thinking about Lacey. Lloyd had come with them to dinner, so he hadn't had a chance to fill Rakesh in on the surreal events of the day. Instead he kept picturing Jenna's pained expression as she talked about her friend, replaying their conversation and trying to shake the creepy feeling that someone had been watching him in the parking lot. He went over his chat with Lacey in his mind, trying to make sense of her requests, which seemed stranger and stranger with every passing minute. Why did she need to take the weekend before she could explain everything? What was she going to explain?

Gabe excused himself to find something to drink, and Jason looked around for someone to talk to. To his left, Kelly Drummond was holding court with a group of guys he might otherwise have joined. To his right, a tight circle of girls whispered to one another. When they erupted in giggles, Jason instinctively smoothed his hair and then patted his face to make sure his glasses were on straight before he saw one of them point to someone making his way down the path. Feeling sheepish, he shoved his hands into his pockets and wandered off.

The clusters were filled with familiar faces. Some he'd known since kindergarten, others he'd seen in the halls but never exchanged words with, but none of them were people he was in the mood to talk to. He checked the time — 11:45. Half an hour before they'd agreed to leave to make Lloyd's curfew.

Jason stepped off the pavement into the shadowy brush, walking until the thumping bass and laughter were nothing more than dull, distant notes. He could hear himself breathing, and he was about to sit on the ground and reread messages from Lacey on his phone when he heard something behind him. He froze. Kids came down this path all the time — to pee, or get away from the party for a minute like he had. The noise was gone, but the skin-crawling sensation of being watched lingered. He turned around slowly and asked, as calmly as he could, "Who's there?" Silence. And then the sound of twigs breaking. He fumbled for his flashlight. It had been a gift from his dad, and though it arrived with the price tag from the Dallas airport still attached, Jason had still slipped it onto his key chain. It had been handy when they were navigating the steep rocky path, but out here its miniature bulb did little more than cast a harsh white glow over the shrubs and branches, illuminating their empty stillness. Was he imagining things? There was no one there. His phone buzzed and he practically jumped out of his skin.

Rakesh: Where'd you go?

Jason told himself he was just being paranoid, but he started back toward the party anyway, until the unmistakable sound of footsteps stopped him dead in his tracks. He pointed the cowboy-boot flashlight and his phone at the same time, shining them in two directions like a gunslinger in a Western. The ghostly pall covered the path, but again, he saw nothing out of the ordinary. *Calm down, Jason,* he thought to himself, *it's been a rough day.* But suddenly out of the corner of his eye he saw movement, and whipped his head toward it so quickly he strained his neck. A figure was speeding up the hill toward the road.

"Hey!" Jason shouted, aiming the flashlight upward. All he could see were shadows, and he started up the incline but tripped on a root, sprawling forward into the dirt. The flashlight snapped off his keys and went flying, its bulb darkening as soon as his grip on it had been released. His phone tumbled out of his hand, casting its ray of light uselessly into the night sky. There was a jolt of pain when his knee came down on a rock, and he cried out. Panicking, he scrambled to his feet, but the figure was gone.

Jason panted and scanned the terrain above him. Nothing but trees. His heart hammered away in his chest, and he tried to get a handle on what had just happened. Alone in the darkness, the person he had seen seemed like a figment of his fearful imagination.

By the time he had limped back to the party, his breathing had evened out, but he garnered a few strange looks for the leaves and dirt stuck to his pants. He hadn't been able to recover the flashlight from whatever bramble it had fallen into — not that he'd lingered a long time searching for it. He was just glad it hadn't been his phone he lost. The kids who noticed whispered to one another, and he realized they thought he'd been in the woods with someone, which probably seemed about as plausible as the idea that he'd been pursued by the reportedly deceased girl from their rival high school.

Just as he found Rakesh, his pocket buzzed again.

"Dude, I'm right here," he said warily. The vibrations from his cell weren't helping Jason's jangled nerves.

"Are you just getting my text now? Yo, you need a new phone. I sent that thing like ten minutes ago. We gotta go if we're gonna get Lloyd home." Rakesh surveyed him, and finally noticed how disheveled he was. "Whoa, where have *you* been?"

But Jason could barely hear him over the rush of blood that rose to his ears when he looked at the text on his iPhone.

Before you start digging around, remember I've got more experience hiding in the dark than you.

The number was blocked.

"C'mon, let's bail," Rakesh was saying, oblivious to Jason. "This party is over anyway."

Jason didn't argue; he was desperate to get out of the woods. They collected Lloyd and trudged up the path to the road. When Jason swung his leg over the guardrail, he was temporarily blinded by the headlights from an oncoming car coming speedily around the curve. The screech of the tires startled Jason and he held his hand up to shield his eyes. He couldn't see the driver, but for a split second he thought he saw a shock of blonde hair. And then the boxy black Volkswagen was speeding away.

The v-dubs is old, but trusty. I call her Vinnie cause she's vintage.

"Jason? You okay?" Lloyd was looking at him strangely, and Jason looked down. He had one leg on either side of the guardrail and his hands gripped it so tightly his knuckles had turned white.

"Uh, yeah," Jason said, hopping over to the road and trying to keep from shivering. "Those headlights just shook me for a second."

"I swear," Lloyd said, "we're lucky no one's been run over yet."

"Seriously," Jason said. But he was barely listening. His mind was back in the woods with his shadowy tail, and hurtling forward with the Volkswagen. It was stuck inside the phone in his pocket. It all seemed so surreal, like a dream, but it was Lacey he'd seen tonight. It had to be. Which meant Lacey was alive He shuddered. It was what he wanted more than anything, so why did he feel like something terrible was about to happen?

CHAPTER 10

*H*ey, buddy! Did you get a haircut? You look great!" Whenever Jason Skyped with his dad, the first question was always about his hair. He wore it the same way day in and day out, with a trim every five weeks, but that didn't make a difference. It was always "Did you get a haircut?" or "I see you're growing out your hair," or once a knowing point to his own head and a suggestive, "Trying something new there, eh?" His dad hated that they only saw each other in person a couple times a year, but Jason wished he'd come up with a better way to express it than commenting on the brown mop Jason did his best to ignore.

"Nope, same hair I always have."

"Well really, it looks great," he repeated. "How's life? How's school? What's new with you?" The barrage of questions was also standard operating procedure for their video chats.

"Life is okay. School is fine. There's not much new." The answer was automatic, and most days it was even true. But a lot had changed in the last week.

"'Okay'? 'Fine'? 'Not much'? Come on, bud, what's new? What's been going on? How's Rakesh? How's *Lacey*?" Jason had forgotten he'd mentioned Lacey to his dad. He hadn't meant to, but a couple weeks ago he'd been so fired up after a particularly great back and forth they had just had regarding Taylor Swift's songwriting abilities (normally averse to all bubblegum pop, Jason had a soft spot for the country star. Lacey was convinced she had a staff of songwriters responsible for her best work) that he dropped her name accidentally when his dad asked what was making him smile.

"Rakesh is good. Colleges keep contacting him about squash. He's thinking about Stanford." Jason didn't know if it was true or not, but he knew his dad wanted him to go to college in California.

"Stanford! That's a great school! I'm in San Francisco all the time for work."

"If Rakesh goes there, you can see him all the time."

"Well, you know how much I like Rakesh, but you're the one I'd like to see all the time. What else is new? What have you been up to this weekend?"

Oh, just visiting my girlfriend's memorial — you know, the one she has because everyone thinks she's dead. I'm getting to know her friends, who like me, and her family, not so much. She won't tell me what's going on, but she is following me and texting me weird messages from strange numbers, so I've got that going for me. "Um, Rakesh and I went to a party last night. I talked to this dude in my class about surfing for a while." He switched gears. "How are you, Dad? How's work? How's Emily?" Emily was his dad's girlfriend. Jason would never tell his mom, but he genuinely liked her.

"I'm all right. Same old, same old at the office — sales calls and meetings and trips up north. Between you and me, I think Emily might kill me if I work late one more time this month. But we're getting by. Are you still thinking you'll come out and visit over spring break?"

"Yeah, but I'll probably have to work for most of the trip — school has been crazy busy." Jason filled his dad in on his classes and listened to him describe a gourmet business dinner he'd had in Napa. Their conversations were always like this — strained at first and then settling into something more comfortable. Jason still wished his dad lived on the East Coast — especially whenever Mark commented on his clothing or tried to bro down with Rakesh — but the hour they spent talking to each other every week was a lot healthier and happier than the relationships some of his friends had with their dads.

When they said good-bye, Jason's head was clear. Feeling inspired, he picked up his notebook, flipping to the back pages where he'd been jotting down lyrics.

> It was all turning gray
> It was all turning black
> Then you were there
> And you keep coming back
>
> These things tend to get ugly
> Or so I am told
> But now that you're here
> Everything's coming up gold
>
> Drive out, see the stars, in the car, we're falling hard
> Wake up, feel the sun, touch your hair, see your heart

He'd pressed his pen to the paper before he fully realized he wasn't on speaking terms with the girl he'd been writing about, because the girl he'd been writing about didn't exist anymore. It wasn't that she was dead — Jason didn't believe that, despite the obituary — but Lacey had a secret, a big one.

At the bottom of the page he'd written

Everything's coming up gold
Everything's coming up gold
Everything's coming up gold

He could hear it in his head. This was how he'd been planning to end the song, but now all he could think about was the blonde hair he'd seen in the darkness the night before. *Just until Monday, I swear. Do you trust me?* It was 4:45 on Sunday afternoon. It would be Monday in no time. But Jason couldn't wait any longer. He tossed away his notebook and opened a new document on his computer.

Lacey,

I don't even know how to say this, but I Googled you last week. I know, I know, kind of stalkerish, but in my defense, I really like you and I just wanted to know more about you. Not the point. You probably know where this is going . . . I found your obituary. And then I found your memorial Facebook page. And then I visited your actual memorial in Brighton Park. And then I called your house.

Jesus, typing this stuff out it seems crazy, and it has FELT crazy. I want to trust you, really, I do, and I want to give you all the time and space you need to figure things out, but you have to admit it's

kind of, um, insane? That everyone thinks you're . . .
dead? You're not dead, right? Because this would be
REALLY weird if you were dead. Haha. Sorry, that's
probably not funny.

Look, I'm sure you have a good reason for all of
this, and whatever it is, I swear, I will be there
for you. I can't even imagine what things must be
like for you that you need to keep these secrets – I
hate the idea that you're in trouble or something.
I think you're great, and I don't want to lose you,
but you have to tell me what's going on or else I
don't know if I can do this anymore.

So, um, that's it. I'm worried about you, and I
want to help you. I hope you write back soon.

    – Jason

PS: Were you following me at the bridge last night?
Or am I just insane? Not sure I want to know the
answer to that one. . . .

Before he could lose his courage, he pasted the message into
Facebook and pressed SEND. He felt a rush of relief that was just
as quickly replaced by anxiety. What if there was a simple, rea-
sonable explanation for her obituary? She would think he was
bonkers. Jason's deepest fear was that the message would scare
her away for good. He couldn't bear the thought of never talking to her again.

He made it all of five minutes without checking to see if she
had responded. She hadn't. He tried to read *Hamlet*, but his
eyes kept wandering up to his computer screen. Sensing he
wasn't going to get anything done, he shut his laptop and

padded downstairs. His mom was sitting in the den reading a magazine. He plopped down next to her.

"Hi, cupcake," she said, looking up at him. "Whatchya doin'?"

"Nothing."

"I've barely seen you this weekend — are you doing okay?"

"I'm fine."

"Is this going to be one of those conversations where all you give me are one-word answers?"

"No."

"But you see my point, right?"

"Mom."

"Because I'm happy to go back to reading my magazine."

"Seriously?"

"Oh, you do one word questions, too?"

"Mom!"

The worst part was that arguing with his mother was still preferable to checking for Lacey's reply. He took a deep breath. "Do you need any help with dinner?"

She eyed him suspiciously. "I know what they say about looking gift horses in the mouth, but are you sure you're okay?"

"Yes, I'm *fine*."

"Well you can set the table. And if you want to eat a salad, you can make one."

He didn't especially want a salad, but chopping cucumbers was something to do. As he worked, he pictured his MacBook morphing into a cartoon mouth, the screen flapping toward the base as it laughed at him, the keys sprouting into jagged rows of teeth.

"You have one new message," it threatened.

An almost-girlfriend everyone thought was dead, dreams about typewriters and quills, shadowy figures in the dark, sketchy text messages from anonymous phone numbers, and now a laptop that could play the villain in a Pixar movie.

Jason wasn't sure how much longer he could live with the sense of creeping dread, with uncertainty about everything, but at least those things had displaced boredom, and Jason didn't much miss his old companion.

CHAPTER 11

*I*t turned out he had to live with the uncertainty for about fifteen hours. He checked Facebook before bed and as soon as he woke up in the morning, but there was not a word from Lacey. And then after chemistry on Monday morning, Jason used his lunch period to duck into the computer lab. There were fifteen Macs there, but three were out of service and four were so old everyone joked they still had dial-up. One of the new ones was free, and Jason plopped down in front of it, greeting Ben Rosenfeld as he settled in.

"Mrs. Kimball's project?" he asked, pointing to the sepia image of Abraham Lincoln he saw on Ben's screen.

"Yeah," Ben said, a bit dolefully. "She gave me a B on the last paper even though I pulled an all-nighter to finish it. I need to ace this one."

Jason nodded sympathetically. He'd gotten an A- and been thrilled, but he knew better than to say anything about it. "She's such a tough grader. I feel like Cynthia's the only person who she consistently gives As to, and that's only because she likes her so much."

"Right? It's so unfair. Are you doing stuff for Kimball's class, too?"

"Uh, yeah," Jason said, eyeing Mr. Hughes, the school's graying technology director. He sat at the entrance to the lab, policing kids who brought open water bottles in and quieting them down when they got too rowdy. He also made sure students only used the computers for official school business. Hughes was tall and skinny. Jason had never seen him wear anything other than khakis, a button-down, and a rumpled tie, and he rarely smiled. Jason navigated to one of Lee's letters, but when he was sure Hughes was fully absorbed in the fantasy scores Jason had seen him checking when he first walked in, he opened a new tab and called up Facebook.

Since freshman year, Facebook and Twitter and any other sites they might actually want to visit had been banned, but it was easy to get around the blocks the school had set up. Jason had been one of the first kids to figure out the trick for getting onto Facebook. When he logged in to his account, there was one new message.

There was no greeting, no playful "what up, dawg?" She was serious.

You weren't supposed to find out this way. I don't want you to get hurt, but now that you've seen what you've seen, I need your help. I didn't disappear because I wanted to. Someone made me, and they will destroy you if they know we're talking.

I know you met Jenna yesterday. I know you didn't tell her anything about me, but I think she can help us. You have to find out if she's my real friend; if we can trust her.

Jason, I'm sorry I lied to you. But you have to know that what's between us is real — the realest thing I have right now — and as complicated as everything else is, you can't doubt that.

"Hey, Jason." Ben's whisper startled him. Expertly, he toggled back to the history page he'd opened, but Ben shrugged as if to say, "I don't care."

"Do you know how many pages our report is supposed to be?"

"I think eight to ten?"

"Thanks. I wish she wasn't so strict about the fonts." Before Jason could reply, they were shushed by Hughes. Jason turned back to his computer, sneaking glances over his shoulder until he was sure Hughes was no longer paying attention.

He reopened Lacey's message and tried to parse it sentence by sentence. She was trying to protect him, but he still didn't understand from what or what was so dangerous. His cheeks burned with shame as he remembered the utter sadness in her father's voice; he wondered if she knew about that, too. He hoped not. And despite all his confusion, his heart swelled as he reread the last lines. *What's between us is real — the realest thing I have right now.* His stomach flipped a little, the way it did before things had gotten so messy, when a message from Lacey was a treat in itself.

He read it again. She didn't say anything about the bridge. What if Lacey hadn't sent the text message he'd gotten on Saturday? *Before you start digging around, remember I've got more experience hiding in the dark than you.* There was something menacing about it, something that didn't sound like Lacey. *They will destroy you if they know we're talking.* Jason felt sick to his stomach. Worrying about Lacey was bad enough, and now there was some mystery third party he had to steer clear of. Who had done this to her? And *what* exactly had they done?

The noise of the bell startled him, and he quickly logged out of Facebook before the other students in the lab could see the letter on his screen. The kids he saw in the halls every day suddenly seemed like potential enemies. Now that Jason had a secret to keep, he wondered what each of them was hiding.

Lunch was his first opportunity to catch up with Rakesh, but as soon as they had settled into their seats in a corner of the cafeteria, Molly Mara attacked. Jason hadn't seen her coming, but when she interrupted his hushed reenactment of his visit to the memorial, he noticed a table full of her girlfriends staring at them and giggling. He flushed, though it was obvious he wasn't the main attraction.

"Hello, *Rakesh*," she said purposefully.

He avoided eye contact. "Hi, Molly."

"I thought we were going to Skype yesterday."

Jason thought of getting up to leave, but he knew Rakesh was desperate not to be left alone with Molly. He'd spent the entire car ride home from the bridge complaining about how she followed him around like a lovesick puppy. More than wanting to support him, Jason wanted to finish his story, so he sat through Rakesh's excuses about the broken camera on his computer, having his phone confiscated by his parents, and getting caught up in a Vince Vaughn marathon on TV. Finally, Molly skulked back to her still-gawking friends. When he was sure she was gone, Rakesh exhaled, adding an exaggerated eye roll.

"Dude, why don't you just tell her you don't like her?"

"I do like her," Rakesh protested, "I just don't want to go to the spring formal with her."

"So tell her that."

"When you meet your girlfriend in person and she can explain why there are obituaries for her everywhere, I will start taking your advice about my love life. Until then, how 'bout you let Rakesh do Rakesh?"

It was Jason's turn to show off his exaggerated eye roll.

"So wait, you met her best friend? Why didn't you tell me at the bridge?"

"I didn't want to bring it up in front of Lloyd. But also . . ." Jason looked around them to make sure no one was listening in. He dropped his voice to a whisper. "I couldn't find you. . . ."

"Yeah, because that one" — he stuck his chin in the direction of Molly's table — "wanted to turn the fact that we kissed *one* time into some huge production."

"Shh! Lower your voice. Can we leave your drama out of this for, like, five minutes?"

Rakesh held up his hands. "Touchy, touchy." He wasn't very sympathetic, but at least he shut up.

"*After* I couldn't find you, I went into the woods. I just wanted some air, but someone followed me."

"Who?"

"I don't know. I mean, I couldn't see them. I thought it was Lacey, but . . ."

"But Lacey's dead?"

"She's not dead!" Several heads swiveled around to see what Jason's outburst was about. When he was sure no one was watching anymore, he resumed his hushed tones and described the message he'd just received. He told Rakesh about his phone call to the Grays, how he impersonated Keith McKeller the guitar teacher and reopened a wound with them. "They definitely have no idea she's alive."

"Are *you* sure she's alive?"

"She messaged me this morning."

"What have our parents been telling us since the day we started using computers? It could be anyone we're talking to online."

"Okay, *Mom*. But this isn't anyone. It's Lacey."

"If you say so. What are you going to do?"

"I have to help her figure out what happened. I'm going to do what she told me and Facebook Jenna."

"Don't you think she's going to be a little bit freaked out to hear that her best friend isn't so dead after all?"

"Not as freaked out as she'll be if we don't get to the bottom of this."

Jason was too distracted by Lacey's message to go to his afternoon classes. Instead, he snuck into the boys' bathroom on the third floor by the music practice rooms. Between its out-of-the-way location and the easily clogged, rarely cleaned toilets, it was almost always deserted. Locking himself in the less disgusting of the two stalls, he took out his phone and logged in to Facebook.

Jenna had hidden most of her profile behind various privacy restrictions, but Jason was still able to recognize her from the thumbnail-size photo depicting her arms wrapped around the shaggy neck of a white sheepdog, her own smooth dark hair framing a huge smile on her face. The third friend that appeared below the photo caught his eye. It was Luke Gray. Jason enlarged the image. He looked a lot like Lacey, but his tanned square jaw and confident gaze at the camera made Jason shrink into himself a little. You could tell he was the type to walk down the hall to class like he was some sort of movie star.

Jason heard footsteps in the hallway and quickly clicked the "Add Jenna Merrick as a friend" button, and then added a message to her.

Hey Jenna,
We met at the memorial in Brighton Park. There's something I want to talk to you about, but I need to do it in person. Can we meet after school one day? I can come to Brighton. OK, thanks.
Jason

He wondered if she'd think he was weird for Facebooking her, if she'd even remember him. But that was the least of his problems. Jenna had the power to break the spell. He was certain the girl he was dealing with online was Lacey and that she was alive, but Jenna knew more about her than anyone in the world. What if she laughed him off? Or told him things about Lacey he didn't want to know? Still, as Jason saw it, he didn't have any other options, so he pressed SEND, watched the bar load on his phone, and then exited the bathroom and made his way to his next class.

Sure enough, when he got home from school, her response was waiting for him.

Hey Jason,

I'm glad you wrote. Maybe it's just 'cause we met at the memorial, but I feel like Lacey would have liked you. Sorry if that is super weird to say . . . I think about her so much though.

Anyway, I will definitely meet up with you. Do you know Play It Again, Sam on Montrose? It's a coffee shop — one of Lacey's favorites. Can you come Wednesday at 4? I'll meet you there.

Jenna

On Wednesday, Jason would go to Lacey's favorite coffee shop and learn all about her life and share a little more about himself. It was just like he'd pictured their first date so many times. The only difference was that in his fantasies, she was there to see it.

CHAPTER 12

*L*acey?"

"Yeah, what was she like?"

Jason settled comfortably into a plush velvety armchair in a corner of Play It Again, Sam. Across from him, Jenna perched on a mismatched overstuffed sofa, her hands wrapped around a steaming latte in a thick homey mug. Over the racket of the espresso machine, notes of Arcade Fire wafted around the softly lit coffee shop. It had a hipster vibe, but it wasn't too pretentious. Of course Lacey liked it. Or would have liked it. He still wasn't sure what tense to use.

Jenna blew gently on her latte before sipping it. After she swallowed, she looked over at him quizzically. "Do you mind if I ask why you want to know?"

Jason had rehearsed this part. He hoped he sounded self-assured rather than wooden, the way he had as a kid when he'd been forced to act in school plays. "Well, I wasn't totally honest with you when we met the other day. I did sort of know Lacey." He watched her closely, but her face was frozen. "I mean, just online. On Facebook. We'd been in touch." Lacey had told him he could confide in Jenna, but Lacey wasn't the one sitting across from her right now, risking everything. If Jason was in danger, he had the right to test the waters before revealing himself to be a complete lunatic.

"When?" Jenna asked coolly.

"A while ago. It wasn't much, but I thought it might turn into something." She nodded without speaking, as if processing the information. "What?" he asked finally.

"I thought it might be something like that," she said. "Part of the reason I came is that I thought you might know something about what happened to her."

Jason felt like his blood had suddenly turned to ice. There was something about the way she said "happened to her" that made him fear he was going to get more of Lacey's story than he wanted to hear. "What do you mean?"

Jenna's eyes narrowed. "When did you say you and Lacey started talking?"

It was his chance to come clean. He'd never liked lying, but he'd played this scene out in his head before he came. Lacey needed to know she could trust Jenna before revealing herself, and Jason did, too — especially if Lacey was right and he was in danger. "It was in the fall," he answered. It wasn't a lie. Not exactly. That was when he first Facebooked her. So what if he didn't hear back until after she faked her own death?

"I see. And how did it start?" Maybe Jason was just being paranoid, but Jenna was starting to resemble a cop conducting an interrogation on a TV show.

"Well, we had the same quote on our profiles. When I noticed it, I messaged her, and then she wrote back. I mean, we barely talked, and it was always about normal stuff, like music or movies. I thought there might be something there, but then she stopped writing me. To be honest with you, I didn't even hear about what happened to her until recently. That's why I went to the memorial."

Jenna didn't say anything, and Jason began fidgeting in his chair. He couldn't tell whether or not she was buying what he was saying. Finally, she responded in a tone so hushed Jason had to lean forward to hear her. "Look, Jason, I think there was something going on with Lacey this fall. Before she, you know . . ."

"Like, what kind of something?"

"I don't know how well you got to know her, but there are things you have to understand about Lacey for this to make sense." She put down her mug and took a deep breath. "It's hard to describe your best friend. The words that come to mind, they're, like, smart, funny, *nice*. Lots of people are smart and funny. Everybody's nice. But Lacey wasn't like a lot of people. She wasn't really like anyone. She had this energy. It was so magnetic. And when you were friends with her, you felt like the coolest person on earth."

She paused to take another sip from her coffee. Warmth had crept into her voice as she talked about Lacey; underneath it, Jason could detect a note of pain. The secret he was keeping tugged guiltily at his heart. "But something changed?"

Jenna looked around nervously. At the other end of the couch was a frazzled, curly-haired woman rocking a baby against her chest while a chubby-cheeked toddler crawled at her feet. A young couple that was thoroughly engrossed in their conversation sat behind him. When she was satisfied no one was watching, she began to explain. "When we got back to school last fall, Lacey seemed . . . different. Like, I'd talk to her about a fight with my mom or something and she'd zone out. And she'd disappear sometimes. We'd have plans, but she'd flake. I'd ask her about it later, and she'd always have some excuse. But I *know* she was hiding something."

"How do you know?" Jason tried to keep the question casual, but he was gripping the handle of his coffee cup tightly.

"Well, it started with the guitar lessons with Max."

"Max?" The name was vaguely familiar, but Jason was certain Lacey had never mentioned a Max. To his surprise, just hearing another guy's name in connection with her made Jason's throat tighten with jealousy.

"He's this guy who goes to our school, and he was teaching Lacey to play. At first I didn't think anything of it. But then she started to spend all her time squeezing in extra lessons or going over to his house to jam. It seemed kind of like something was going on."

"I take it she, um, didn't have a boyfriend?" Jason's voice cracked on the last word, and he quickly raised his drink to his lips so Jenna wouldn't see his face color. He hadn't bargained on Lacey being involved with some rock-star type. He silently vowed to finish the song he'd been working on so he could show it to her when they met. *If* they met.

"It figures you would ask that," Jenna said, rolling her eyes. Her tone was playful, but Jason wondered if there was bitterness in it, too. She continued, "No, she was single, and Max *so* isn't her type, which is why it was so weird that she was supposedly spending all her time with him."

"So you think she was using the guitar stuff as a cover for something?"

"That's sort of why I wanted to see you when you e-mailed me. I thought you might know something about what she was hiding. I thought you might even *be* something she was hiding. No offense."

He shook his head no, and the look of disappointment on her face pained Jason so much that part of him wanted to confess everything. Lacey had told him to find out if Jenna was her real friend. There was no doubt in Jason's mind that she was. Before he could open his mouth, though, Jenna started to cry. He'd seen girls cry before, of course. In school when someone got an unexpected bad grade, or on a Friday night after fighting with a friend, girls had broken down, but none of them had ever cried alone with him like this. They'd sobbed to one another or to guys like Rakesh, while Jason pretended not to stare from a safe distance away. For a second, Jason froze where he was, but then he gingerly moved to the seat next to her on the couch and patted her shoulder. She leaned into him, and he put an arm awkwardly around her. "Oh god," Jenna sniffled, "this is so embarrassing."

"You have nothing to be embarrassed about. I'm sorry if I said something that upset you."

She wiped away tears. "It's not you. It's just . . . ugh, I don't know how to say this without making you think I'm crazy."

He sensed she was about to say something big. Was she going to tell him she thought Lacey was still alive? His pulse quickened, and he feared she'd be able to hear his heart beating through his shirt. He kept his voice steady when he informed her, "I won't think you're crazy. I swear."

She looked up at him, water pooling in the corners of her hazel eyes. He could hardly breathe. And then she cast her glance downward. "I just keep thinking about that night," she sighed.

"Oh." The word was hollow and his shoulders went slack. Of course she didn't think her friend was alive. He tried to hide his disappointment. But it was still an opportunity to learn more about what had happened to Lacey and who had done it. "We don't have to talk about it if you don't want, but, like, what happened to her? Has anyone figured it out?"

Jenna inhaled raggedly. "Everything had been so weird. And then the night of Roxy Choi's party, she looked like she hadn't slept in a week. We'd barely seen each other in school, and when I saw her she hugged me really hard. I thought she was finally going to tell me what was going on, and I was so relieved. I hated feeling like we were in a fight because neither of us can stand drama. Could stand drama. God, I don't even know how to talk about her anymore."

Her shoulders heaved with another round of sobs, but she didn't stop talking. "That night at Roxy's, I thought things were going to go back to normal, and then she went to say hi to someone and I lost track of her. I looked for her, but I couldn't find her. Eventually, I had to leave to make my curfew. Then when I didn't hear from her that weekend, I got so angry."

She buried her head in her hands, and Jason rubbed her back. When she could speak again, she continued, "I just . . . I really miss her. I hate myself for being mad at her after that party. I know I'm obsessing, but I can't stop thinking about that night. I wish I had found her before I left. I know it's crazy, but I'm getting this weird vibe, like I could have changed something."

"I'm sure whatever was going on with her wasn't about you." *She loves you*, he wanted to add. *You and I, we're the only people she trusts.* Now more than ever he was sure Lacey had a good reason for hiding, and they were going to figure it out together. He just had to tell Lacey Jenna was on their side. Instinctively, he reached for her hand, and she squeezed it gratefully.

"It's just . . . I've been on Roxy Choi's balcony, and you have to be pretty clumsy to fall off it backward. The upstairs was off-limits — I don't even know why she would have been up there in the first place. Maybe I'm just obsessing over it, but I feel like I'm missing part of the story."

"You're not obsessing. And none of this sounds crazy. You miss your friend — that's really normal. I can't even imagine going through what you've been through."

For the first time since she arrived, she smiled. "Honestly, it feels really good to talk. With her gone, I've been keeping all this stuff to myself, and I didn't realize how badly I needed to get it out."

Jason wished he could tell her how much he agreed. Instead he told her she could talk to him anytime. "Seriously, I'm always free. Text me, call me."

"Thank you for not thinking I'm crazy. I really feel like I can trust you."

Pushing everything he wasn't telling her to the back of his mind, he looked her dead in the eye and responded, "You can."

CHAPTER 13

When Jason got home, he immediately fired off a message to Lacey informing her about his meeting with Jenna. "We can trust her," he wrote. "I'm sure of it." After clicking SEND, his mind was quieter, and he brushed his teeth and climbed into bed. He wasn't sure how long he'd been asleep when something woke him. Jason sat up groggily. His limbs were heavy with sleep, and his mouth felt like it was filled with cotton. He cursed himself for forgetting to bring a glass of water to bed.

He tiptoed to the kitchen, the tile smooth against his bare feet, and opened the refrigerator door, blinking furiously when the light from within flooded the room. He poured himself water and drank it in one gulp, then refilled the glass and leaned against the counter to sip it slowly. He heard the stairs creak under the weight of footsteps and his shoulders stiffened guiltily — being out of bed in the middle of the night still made him feel like a little kid. He waited for his mom or Mark to appear in the doorway, but neither did. After a few moments of nothing more than stillness and silence, Jason told himself he was imagining things, and some of the tension eased out of his neck.

He filled his cup one last time and returned to his room, pausing when he saw the glow of his laptop open on his desk. Of course, he'd left it on overnight before, but he hadn't noticed it when he woke up originally. When he thought back now, though, he couldn't remember shutting it after messaging Lacey. He gently lowered the top and then crawled back under his blankets, pulling them tightly around him.

This time sleep didn't come easily. His afternoon with Jenna was still fresh in his memory, and he turned her words over in his mind, wondering what he was missing. What secret was so dark Lacey had to hide it from her best friend? Knowing he had to get up in a few hours, he tried to push the questions from his mind, and willed himself to count sheep instead. Gradually, visions of fluffy white farm animals quieted his brain, and his muscles surrendered to slumber.

And then through the darkness he heard something rustling and bolted up in bed.

"Who's there?" he asked, his voice thick. He squinted into the dark room, but without his glasses it was all blurry.

His inquiry was met with deathly quiet, but something in Jason's gut told him he wasn't alone. He thought back to the creaking from the staircase. There was an intruder in the house — in his *room*. He knew he should get out of bed, flick on the light switch, see who — or what — was there, but fear had immobilized him. His blood pulsed violently in his ears when he heard the distinct sound of breathing. In the darkness, he couldn't tell where it was coming from.

"I've got a baseball bat." Jason meant it to sound like a warning, but it came out in a shaky whisper. He might as well have added, "And it's somewhere in the basement."

His skin went clammy, and he wondered if he was having a nightmare. The breathing sound was gone, there was no more rustling. His vision had finally adjusted to the darkness, and nothing appeared to be out of the ordinary, but just to be safe, he groped for the lamp, illuminating his empty room. His door was shut, the window closed. To be safe, he peered under the bed and gasped with fright before he realized the beast that scared him was only a dust bunny that had gathered on one of his shoes, moving in the breeze. *Calm down, Jason,* he told himself. *Now you're just hallucinating things.* He switched off the light and waited for his own breathing to settle. Turning onto his side, he told himself it had only been a dream. He closed his eyes and tried to summon visions of the puffy, peaceful sheep that had comforted him a few minutes before, but he knew he'd only spend the rest of the night tossing and turning.

Finally, he swung his legs out of bed, slid on his glasses, and settled at his desk, switching on his desk lamp. He wanted to see if Lacey had answered his message, but as he waited for Facebook to load, something caught his eye and made him freeze in his seat. The white border of a photograph was resting on top of an open notebook. He hadn't left a photograph there. He never even got photos printed. Cautiously, he reached for it, sliding it toward himself carefully as if it might explode, or worse, turn to dust in his hands.

It depicted two people leaning against a chain-link fence beneath a brilliant blue sky. It was taken from some distance away, but he knew instantly that one of them was Lacey. He blinked and then pinched his wrist. Was he dreaming? Had he *not* been imagining things when he'd heard the rustling in his room, the creaking on the stairs?

He looked frantically around the room, and when he was sure there was no one else present, he examined the photograph closely. It was a candid shot. Lacey's soft golden waves fell around her face, her eyes trained straight ahead. She was wearing a loose white T-shirt, a gray-and-red-striped skirt with bare legs and tennis shoes, and stood next to a tall guy in a bright red-and-white Brighton varsity jacket. He wore his light brown hair cropped short, and even from far away, you could tell he had the chiseled features girls stayed up at night thinking about.

They weren't looking at each other, but there was something about the *way* they were avoiding each other's gaze, about their purposefully casual posture and ultracomposed facial expressions, that made it look like they were in the middle of an intense and secretive conversation.

I know *she was hiding something.* Jenna's words echoed in his ears.

Jason snatched at the notebook it had been resting on. Maybe there would be some sort of note or explanation. What he saw made his heart drop. Inside the spiral binding, there was the scrap of paper where the sheet had been ripped away. Immediately, he knew which page. The song. The one he'd been writing for Lacey. He tore through the notebook, but it was gone. Whoever had been there had taken it. He overturned every item on his desk, and riffled through the pages of his textbooks, but there was no other trace of his predawn visitor.

Remember I've got more experience hiding in the dark than you.

Someone was watching Jason, that much was obvious, but it terrified him to think of who. Other than Rakesh, the only person who knew about him and Lacey *was* Lacey. Was she the one who'd snuck in? He'd thought about her in his bedroom before, but in his imagination what unfolded bore no resemblance to the surreal events that had just taken place.

He tried to slip into room 207 unnoticed, but Mrs. Kimball paused her recitation of the morning announcements and turned to the door with pursed lips. Though Jason hadn't fallen back asleep, he'd been slow to tear himself away from his computer when his alarm clock alerted him it was time to get ready for school. Instead he'd clicked refresh on his messages over and over again to see if Lacey had written anything, and as he dressed he kept his eye glued to the corner of the screen to see if her name would appear with a green dot next to it. Jason mumbled his apologies and slid into the only open desk. He cursed himself for being late. Now he had no prayer of not getting caught if he checked his phone for a response from Lacey.

As soon as the first-period bell rang, Rakesh sidled up next to him.

"Missed you in the student lounge this morning."

The hallways were full of teachers. His phone would get confiscated before he could even open Facebook. "Yeah, I overslept."

"Oooh, big night out with Lacey's friend?"

"What?" Jason said blankly before he remembered he'd told Rakesh he was meeting Jenna. "No. I mean, sort of."

"Why are you being so shady?"

Without realizing it, he'd been whispering. He'd thought Jenna's secret-agent act at the coffee shop had been a bit overdone, but now he worried they hadn't been secretive enough.

"Can you meet up after school today?" Jason kept looking over his shoulder. "I'll explain everything."

"You're like *I Love Lucy* with all this 'splaining, and I'm getting tired of playing Ricardo, even if we are both fine brown men. I want in on some of the action."

"Oh my god, are you seriously quoting *I Love Lucy* to me right now?"

"What? I love me some Nick at Nite. Nothing wrong with that."

"Can you meet up after school?"

"Will you admit that you are definitely Ethel?"

"Rakesh!"

"Fine, not only are you basically a total pansy, but you also have no sense of humor sometimes. But I am a good friend, so I will meet you in the parking lot after last period. Are you happy now?"

The girl of his dreams was in hiding or worse. Maybe she'd been in his room last night, or maybe a total stranger had. "Nothing would bring me more joy," he answered coldly.

Molly Mara was leaning against the hood of Jason's car, her palms spread flat behind her. In a low-cut tight purple dress and lacy black tights, she laughed with her mouth wide open and her head back, like she was offering her neck up to some hungry vampire. Molly swung her hair forward and straightened her face before looking straight into Rakesh's eyes and telling him seriously, "You're so funny, you should be a comedian."

"Never heard that one before." Jason grumbled the words under his breath, but it was still louder than he intended. Molly and Rakesh both looked up guiltily, as if they'd been caught breaking school rules. Come to think of it, Jason was pretty sure Molly's outfit was a dress-code violation.

"Hi, Jason!" Molly spoke in an enthusiastic singsong. "Rakesh was just telling me how good you are at Grand Theft Auto."

"Actually, I was telling her how much better I am."

Molly laughed again, and Jason glared at Rakesh, who just shrugged. It wasn't his fault he shone like a candle to Roosevelt's female population of moths. When nobody spoke, Molly straightened up and shook out her hair.

"I guess I should let you two boys go be boys. I'll see you later, Rakesh."

"OMG you are just *so* hilarious," Jason mimicked when she was out of earshot.

"Yeah, I *am* hilarious, don't hate."

"Whatever." Jason was sullen as he started the car. He hadn't been able to check Facebook until last period, and Lacey's message had been brief.

I knew I could count on you. Tell Jenna about me. She might be freaked out, but you have to make her understand. If she doesn't believe you, ask her if she still has the penguin's shirt in the back of her closet. And tell her I'm so, so sorry I can't talk to her myself—tell her I'm sorry about everything.

There was no mention of being in his room, no enlightening backstory about the photo. He knew hearing from Lacey at all was a good sign, but she wasn't helping with Jason's confusion.

It was too strange to be relieved she hadn't said anything about the song.

"Okay, what is up with you?" Rakesh asked angrily. "You won't tell me anything, and now you're mad because Molly likes me?"

"I don't care that Molly likes you. I just have stuff going on."

"I'm trying to help you! What even happened yesterday?"

Jason recounted his coffee with Jenna as he navigated the familiar streets of Oakdale, and then he began to describe the strange nighttime encounter. By the time he was done with the story, they were both slumped on the sofa in Jason's den.

"Can I see the photo?" Rakesh said.

Jason handed it over and watched his friend study it.

"Lacey's got nice legs," Rakesh observed before Jason snatched it back, taking his own turn trying to extract some meaning from the image in his hands. The guy gave Jason the creeps. The photo had to have something to do with the secret Lacey had been keeping.

"When are you going to tell Jenna?" Rakesh asked finally, his tone conciliatory.

"I was going to text her when you left, but if you're going to sit on my couch all night, I'll do it now."

"You're going to tell her Lacey's alive over text?"

Jason paused. "I'll see if she has a Skype log-in. Is that better?"

Rakesh turned on the TV and started flipping through channels, but when the response came through on Jason's phone, he took his eyes off *The Real Housewives* and looked down at the screen.

I have to wait until my parents go to bed, but my Skype is jennayeahyeahyeah. Midnight?

"A midnight Skype date with a lady," Rakesh observed. "If I didn't know better, I'd start to think you had some game, Jason Moreland."

Game was one thing, but a game plan was a whole other. He had to figure out a way to make his omissions about Lacey's ongoing presence in his life not seem like a betrayal. More important, he had to keep Jenna from thinking he was a complete lunatic. In the end, he decided to keep it simple.

In the den with the door shut tightly, he balanced his laptop on his knees and placed his oversize headphones over his ears. At the stroke of twelve, he opened a connection with Jenna.

"Hey." She waved, and giggled. She was wearing pajamas, a T-shirt with the neckline cut wide like an '80s pop star, and a green terry-cloth headband pulled her hair back from her face. It was like they were at a slumber party together. "Sorry about this. My parents don't really like me being online during the week unless it's for school. I can get away with Facebook, but video is harder."

"I know the feeling," Jason said, double-checking that the lights in the next room were still off.

"So what's up?" she asked.

He knew there was no easy way to break the news. He was too tired and confused — too desperate for answers — to dance around what he had to say. So he took a deep breath and went for it. "I haven't been totally honest with you. About Lacey. I'm sort of . . . still in touch with her."

"Uh, what do you mean?" she asked nervously.

"Lacey and I, we started e-mailing in February. And we've been talking since then." He had to force himself to watch her reaction as he spoke. Her mouth was beginning to turn down around the edges, and he could see confusion in her eyes.

"I don't understand. Lacey's dead. She died in October."

"I know everybody thinks that, but there's something going on. At first she told me not to tell anyone, that's why I didn't say anything, but she says we can trust you."

"Jason." She was shaking her head. "Stop it. This is sick."

"Please, Jenna, you told me yourself, you think you're missing something. The thing you're missing is that she's not gone."

"I told you that in confidence, because I *trusted* you. I thought . . . I thought you were a nice guy." He had longed for a girl to think of him as something more than just a nice guy, but this wasn't what he'd bargained for.

"Just let me explain. There's a chance she's still alive. Don't you want to know what I know? Don't you want to figure out the truth?"

"The truth?" There was outrage in her voice. "You're going to talk to me about the truth? I don't even know who you are. How am I supposed to believe anything you say? Talking to you . . . this was a huge mistake, Jason. I'm sorry." She started to take out her earbuds, and he could see her reaching for the button to end the conversation.

He only had one chance. He took a deep breath and blurted it out. "Do you still have the penguin's shirt in the back of your closet?"

She froze. "What did you just say?"

"The penguin's shirt. Do you still keep it at the back of your closet?"

"Who told you to say that to me?"

"Lacey."

"This isn't funny. Who told you that? How do you know about that?"

"I *know* it isn't funny. That's what I'm trying to tell you. There's something going on. I need your help figuring out what. Lacey needs both of us to help her."

She sat back against the couch. Jason couldn't tell whether Lacey's plan had worked until Jenna crossed her arms, leaned forward, and said into the camera, "Okay, I'm listening."

He started at the beginning, with the original message, and the response months later, the discovery of the obituary and the double profile, the strange confrontation in the woods, and the photo he'd found in his bedroom that morning. Jenna listened intently, occasionally interrupting with questions about what Lacey had said to him, until he told her everything. Well, almost everything. He didn't go into much detail regarding his feelings for Lacey and his deep, sincere hope that he hadn't totally misjudged the situation. "So do you believe me now?" he asked when he finished.

She exhaled slowly. "It's a lot to take in."

"I know."

"I mean, I *want* it to be true. Like, more than anything. But, the body they found . . ." She trailed off, and Jason felt vaguely sick, like he had when he'd first found the obituary. He'd been too scared to ask — until now.

"Yeah, about that," he said, "is there a chance it was a mix-up? That it was someone else?"

"I don't know the details," Jenna answered. "When we got the news, everything was so awful. The only thing I really remember from that week is crying all the time, and when I've seen the Grays since then, it hasn't seemed appropriate to ask about the details." She paused thoughtfully, biting her lip and staring intently into the camera. "I don't understand why she didn't message me or call me. Or why she disappeared."

Relief flooded Jason when he realized he could offer her some comfort on this point. "She wanted me to tell you she's sorry she can't talk to you herself. She said she was sorry for everything." When Jenna looked at him, he could see the hope in her eyes. "I don't understand it all, either. But we can figure it out. I think the photo I found in my room is a clue." He held the picture up to the camera. "Do you have any idea who this is with Lacey?"

"That's Troy," she said, her puzzlement written all over her face. "He's her brother's best friend. You found that in your room?"

"I think Lacey left it for me."

"But you don't know why."

"No. And I haven't had a chance to Facebook her and ask. We need to find her, though. Do you have any ideas how we do that?"

"I'm still trying to adjust to the idea that she's alive some-where." She paused. "There is actually someone."

"Who's that?"

"Max. Her guitar teacher."

"I don't know . . ." Jason's hesitance to get anyone else involved was outweighed by his desire to find Lacey. Finally, he consented. "But promise me you'll be careful," Jason said.

"With her family, too, if you talk to them. You say Luke is harmless, but I don't get that impression."

"I promise," she said, punctuating the statement with a big yawn. "I won't tell him anything. But he cared about her. Maybe he'll know something that will help us."

"I'll let you go to bed," he said. The clock in the corner of his screen read 1:24. Tomorrow was going to be rough. "But I want you to know I'm really sorry."

Jenna looked confused. "For what?"

"I wanted to tell you all of this in the coffee shop. I just didn't know if it was safe."

"If Lacey trusts you, then I trust you," she answered firmly.

The words lifted an enormous weight from his shoulders. He had been feeling like a jerk for keeping this from her — not to mention he was terrified she wouldn't believe him. "Thanks. You have no idea how much that means to me. Oh yeah, I meant to ask you, what's the whole 'the penguin's shirt' thing about?"

The warm grin returned to her face. "I'll tell you one day, if you're lucky."

He laughed. "Oh, just what I need, another mystery."

CHAPTER 14

It was Sunday afternoon when Jason felt the panic seep back in. School on Friday had been sluggishly slow, and in the evening, exhausted from his Thursday night Skype session with Jenna, he popped his *Goonies* DVD into his computer, collapsed into bed, and swiftly fell asleep. Saturday he'd gone to a record fair, blowing half the cash he had saved on a rare Pixies LP. It was a good investment as far as he was concerned. He placed it on his turntable as soon as he got home, and whiled away the evening creating iTunes playlists based around lost gems from 1989. He woke Sunday morning to gray weather, ate cereal from the box, and chugged OJ from the carton, and then crawled back under his covers with his now-battered copy of *Hamlet*.

By Ophelia's suicide, the play had become so gripping that Jason barely moved as he read, speeding through the grave-digger's riddles and her funeral until all of Denmark's royal court lay in a bloody heap. Poisoned, killed by their own treachery, murdered in cold blood. And they didn't even have Facebook to deceive one another with.

His stomach was growling when he finished the fifth act, and as he padded downstairs in search of lunch, visions of Lacey filled his head. It had been radio silence since he'd written her about his conversation with Jenna. It was just a short note, telling her Jenna knew, assuring her they would help, and asking what, specifically, she wanted them to do. And then nothing. He was starting to get nervous. What if something had happened to her? Something worse than whatever had caused her to disappear in the first place.

While he waited for the leftover pasta he found in the fridge to reheat, he opened his laptop on the kitchen counter and began to type. He got as far as "Dear Lacey" before the microwave beeped.

"Who's Lacey?" Jason hadn't heard his mom come in the kitchen. He spun around and pushed the top of his laptop down.

"Mom! A little privacy?"

"What? It was open in *my* kitchen."

He glared at her.

"Touchy, touchy," she said, holding her hands up in surrender. "Moving on. Don't eat too much of that spaghetti, my little meatball. Mark's grilling chicken for dinner."

It was later in the afternoon than he'd realized, but just to make a point he hoisted an enormous forkful of noodles into his mouth and chewed dramatically. "Sure thing," he said sweetly with his mouth still full.

"You're adorable. Totally adorable. Seriously, though, if you don't put that bowl in the dishwasher when you're done with it, I really will take this away for a month." She tapped his laptop menacingly.

"Fine," he said once he'd swallowed. "Besides, when do I not clean up after myself?"

"Ha! Good one, muffin. Look, I can tell you're doing the whole, 'I'm a sullen teenager' thing today, so I'm gonna get out of your way. But pull it together before dinner, 'cause I'm really not in the mood for any more of this."

She was right that he was being immature, but he was so annoyed both that she looked at his computer and that she was patronizing him that he rolled his eyes as soon as she turned her back. Still, when he'd finished off the pasta, he took care to rinse the bowl and load it into the dishwasher, and washed the empty coffeepot that was sitting in the sink for good measure. Then, laptop under his arm, he returned to the safety of his room.

Sitting down to write, he wished for the gazillionth time that things with him and Lacey could be simple. He wanted so badly to brag about the album he'd scored the day before and send her the playlists he'd made. He'd been scratching new lyrics to the song he was writing in his notebook, reciting them aloud and crossing them out when they sounded clunky or cheesy or wrong. He was determined to write a song she would love, and the desire to impress her felt strange considering he had bigger problems than being liked. Despite all of her warnings about how they were in danger, he kept picturing them going to the spring formal together. But there'd be no chance of that if he didn't figure out how to help her soon.

Lacey,

I'm worried about you. I'm sure you have a good reason for not answering my note, but I'm really lost right now. I went to Jenna like you asked — I mean, you know that already — and now I feel like I'm waiting for something, but I don't even know what.

And . . . were you in my room? I didn't bring it up because I thought it was a dream. But it wasn't, was it? Don't take this the wrong way, but I have thought about you in my room before, but usually when I

imagine it you don't just disappear. Did you leave
that photo? Gahhh, I'm sorry I keep sending you these
questions, but I feel like I don't know anything
anymore.

If you're still there, please just answer this and
let me know you're all right. Let me know what I can
do to help you. I hope you know you can trust me.
Really. Whatever you want. You just have to ask
for it.

– J

He thought about asking the obvious question. *Are you still
alive?* but it seemed too absurd. Mostly, though, he didn't want
to consider the possibility that she wasn't. If Lacey Gray was
dead, then what was it all for? He took a deep breath, and
clicked SEND.

Though Jason would never tell Mark to his face, he secretly
loved his stepdad's cooking. The chicken was juicy and flavor-
ful, and Jason tore into a drumstick like he hadn't eaten in
weeks. He'd finished the pasta to spite his mom, but his stomach could barely tell the difference. He had just shoved three
quarters of a buttered roll into his mouth when she asked, "So
seriously, Jason, who's Lacey?"

"She's a friend," he said carefully once he'd swallowed.

"Lacey's a nice name," Mark chimed in. "Are you two . . .
you know." He raised his eyebrows suggestively, and Jason shot
him a withering glance. It was bad enough when his real dad
asked after her politely.

"We're just friends," he said firmly.

"Does she go to Roosevelt?"

He could tell his mom she went to Brighton. It wasn't exactly true, but it was close. He hated being dishonest with his mother because she rarely lied about anything. Even when he was little she would always level with him. But they didn't talk about girls much at the dinner table — or at all — so Jason knew the more details he gave the more questions she would have. If he said Brighton, she would want to know how they had met and why he was writing her. And what if she had somehow heard about Lacey's death?

On second thought, maybe lying wasn't such a bad idea. "Uh, yeah. We're working on a chem project together."

"I thought Rakesh was your lab partner."

"He is. It's just that this is a group project, so me and Rakesh are working with Lacey and her partner . . . Jenna." Before his mom could pick up on the second unfamiliar name, Jason charged onward. "Actually, we're going to need to work on it after school a couple days this week. So I might not be home for dinner. I may wind up staying out kind of late."

"Maybe Karen and I can do some chemistry experiments of our own while you're out." Mark laughed at his own joke loudly. Jason's mom joined in.

"Um, gross." Jason pushed his food away. It was disgusting, but at least it had ended the conversation. "May I be excused?"

Jason was actually looking forward to English class. He hadn't been able to stop thinking about *Hamlet*, even if most of those thoughts revolved around the parallels to his own situation with Lacey. He'd highlighted and underlined and circled so many different lines and passages that the play would be virtually useless to someone else who was trying to read it.

"The fool seems like a Gatsby-esque figure to me," Dave Jordan started obnoxiously, and Jason stifled a groan.

Apparently even Mrs. Granger had grown tired of the Gatsby references. "I think we've covered Fitzgerald well enough. Let's focus on the Shakespeare in front of us. What is the clown saying in this scene?"

In the margins of his book, Jason had written, "death is certain," and underlined it three times. For all the subtleties in his work, sometimes the Bard was pretty straightforward. He raised his hand, and Mrs. Granger suppressed a smile when she called on him.

"*Delighted* to hear from someone new. Yes, Jason?"

"When he says, 'the houses he makes lasts till doomsday,' he's not joking, even if it is part of that riddle. I don't really think anything he says is supposed to be a joke, even if some of it is funny."

"Yes, excellent. And as I'm sure you all realized reading the footnotes, 'clown' is not a scary guy with big shoes, a painted face, and bozo hair — the closest parallel to that is Yorick, the jester whose skull Hamlet gets philosophical with. Here, though, 'clown' is just a term he's using for a country bumpkin type with a wicked sense of humor. Jason, can you talk about why he's the one Shakespeare wanted delivering these lines?"

"Well it's foreshadowing," Jason continued, blushing inwardly at his use of one of the literary terms Dave and Katie were prone to abuse, "because really everybody in this play is about to die." The class laughed. "I mean, this is coming right in between a suicide and a bloodbath. If he'd had a character say this stuff seriously, it would have been way too heavy-handed — not to mention a total downer. It doesn't make what's going to happen funny, but it makes it, like, okay. Kind of like what Hamlet is saying about death being inevitable and life being something more than just having a body. If that makes any sense."

She beamed at him. "It certainly does. Let's talk about what Hamlet is saying," she said to the class. "Do you guys think there's anything strange about it?"

Relieved that his contribution to the class had not been disastrous, Jason withdrew and reconsidered some of what he'd said. It had sounded solid, and Granger had gone for it, but he felt a cold hollowness in his chest when he thought about Lacey's life being over. Just because she was going to die someday didn't mean he was okay with her dying right now, regardless of clever riddles. He shouldn't have opened his mouth. It was just like everything else in his life lately: Whenever he thought he knew something for sure, it turned out he knew even less than he thought was possible. Just then, something Katie was saying caught his attention.

"Hamlet's always going on and on about his inner turmoil, but he doesn't feel any guilt or even any responsibility for Ophelia."

"Should he?" Mrs. Granger asked.

"Well he basically *killed* her," Katie said definitively.

"How do you figure that?" Dave challenged.

"He murdered Polonius, and that's why she killed herself. So he's responsible."

"He could plead temporary insanity to Polonius."

"Yeah, except he keeps trying to tell everyone he's not crazy!"

"But he still didn't *kill* Ophelia."

"If he's so torn up over her death, why doesn't he see that he was involved in it?"

"Take it easy, you two," Mrs. Granger interrupted. "This doesn't need to turn into debate club. You're both bringing up interesting questions, and we're running out of time for today. For tomorrow, can y'all think about this question: What does it mean to be responsible for someone's death? Good class today, everyone."

Jason copied down the words as blood rushed in his ears. He felt so powerless when it came to Lacey. He wanted to protect her, but he had no clue how to do that. But what if he had the situation all wrong? What if he was only making things worse for her?

Oblivious to Jason's own inner turmoil, Mrs. Granger caught his arm on his way out of the classroom. "Jason, thank you for participating in the discussion today. I love a fresh perspective. I hope you won't let the brawl at the end discourage you from speaking up again." She winked at him like he was a coconspirator. He stammered his thanks and made his way out into the hallway in a daze. Out of habit, he checked his phone as he walked to his next class. There was a text from Jenna.

Need to talk ASAP. Can you meet after school? I'll come to Oakdale.

He should have been happy. He was going to get some answers soon, but he wasn't sure he wanted them anymore.

CHAPTER 15

At a small table at Michael's, Pete Schmidt and Camille Piangiani were breaking up. They had been together since sophomore year, and Pete still loved Camille, but when he started at the University of Colorado next year, he didn't want to be thinking about someone in Chicago. It was a scoop any Roosevelt High student would have bragged about getting, and on a normal day, Jason would have claimed credit for breaking the news, but he hadn't even noticed them sitting down in the booth next to him. Instead, he stared straight ahead as the words "Lacey had a secret boyfriend" drowned out all the other noise in the room.

When Jenna had arrived at Michael's, she'd introduced Max, a tall, dark-haired boy with pale wrists poking out of a leather jacket and string-bean legs clad in stiff skinny jeans. Before Jason could ask what he was doing there, Jenna slid into the booth and urgently whispered the news to him. As he heard it, he felt the earth tilt under him, as if any moment the three of them, complete with their booth, would slide away, like deck chairs on the *Titanic*. The weirdest part was that he felt even more betrayed than he had when he found the obituary. He told himself it was silly — he was overreacting, and slowly his vision righted itself. The booth wasn't going anywhere. Like so many other things, this was just a misunderstanding.

"I'm sorry, what are you doing here?" His eyes were locked on Max and his own voice sounded unfamiliar.

In another life, Jason and Max could have been friends. In another life, they could have met up at shows and traded playlists, even started a band together. But right now, in this restaurant, Jason was filled with angry envy that Max had spent time with Lacey, had seen the light of day move across her face and the swing of her hair, the movement of her arms.

"Jason, can we talk in private for a second?" Jenna asked as she rose from her seat.

Jason nodded, hoping a moment away from the table would help clear his head. When they stepped outside, the icy March air hit him like a slap in the face. He had to stop sulking.

"We have to tell him what's going on."

"We can't," Jason protested. "I promised her we wouldn't tell anyone." As he said it, a tide of anger swelled inside of him. He'd agreed to keep Lacey's secret, but she'd conveniently omitted the one that hurt Jason the most.

"I know you did. But he's going to be more helpful to us if he knows the whole truth."

"Lacey's in danger. Until we know who made her disappear, we can't tell *anyone*."

"Max is different. He'd never hurt anyone. And we can trust him. All of his friends are musicians in the city — he barely talks to anyone at school. I'm sure he'll keep anything we tell him on the DL."

Maybe it was the boyfriend Lacey had concealed from him, or maybe it was the way Jenna looked at him with those pleading hazel eyes, but Jason felt his resolve soften. "You're positive about this?"

"Yes. Look, I wouldn't do this if I thought it might put Lacey in any more danger than she's already in. Whatever Max knows about her is going to help us figure out where she is and keep her safe."

"Okay," Jason said at last. He was tired of hiding things, tired of arguing.

When they got back inside the diner, the food they'd ordered was waiting for them on the table. Max put away his phone when they slid back into the booth. "So," he said, picking up a french fry, "are you guys going to let me in on the secret?"

Jenna and Jason exchanged a glance. He signaled for her to go ahead.

"I guess that was sort of obvious," she sighed. "I'm sorry. Look, Max, there's something you should know, but you have to swear you're not going to tell anyone what we tell you."

"So I can't put this on my blog?" he asked in mock disappointment.

"This is serious. Can we trust you?"

"Yeah," he said, the sarcasm gone.

"All right." She took a deep breath. "Remember how I told you Jason and Lacey were Facebook friends?" He nodded. "They've been talking since *after* Roxy's party."

"Wait, you mean you're communicating with her in the afterlife?" The question was equal parts skepticism and confusion.

"No," Jason answered, adding quietly, "Lacey's still alive."

"Um, I hate to be the one who has to tell you this, but you sound kind of insane."

"He's not," Jenna answered sharply. "Listen, Lacey's not gone. She's hiding somewhere. I know you're not telling me everything you know."

He looked chastened. "Okay," he said slowly. "But why should I believe you?"

Jason let Jenna tell it. He was grateful for the opportunity to tune out for a few minutes. He picked at the fries on the table, but his mind was somewhere else, somewhere where he didn't have to compete with some mystery guy for Lacey's affection. He told himself he was overreacting — it's not like they were technically together and she hadn't promised him anything — but it did little to soothe the knot of jealousy that was twisting in his gut.

Max's deep voice interrupted Jason's internal monologue. "How can you be sure it's actually Lacey?"

"Wild Flag made her favorite album of last year. She sings Robyn at the top of her lungs when she's alone in her car. You were teaching her to play 'No Children' on the guitar, except she was getting tripped up in the first verse."

Max looked stunned, and then turned to Jenna for a response. "It's true," she said. "Trust me, I was as freaked out as you look right now, but she told Jason things about me only she could have known."

There was a long pause during which Jason decided he didn't care whether or not Max believed them. But when Max finally said, "You're right, I didn't tell you everything," he felt validated in a small way.

"It didn't seem like my place," Max continued, "I barely knew her before that summer. I mean, when she came up to me in school last year and asked if I would teach her to play the guitar, I thought it might be some sort of joke. Lacey was nice and all, but between her brother and her friends, I was pretty sure she was a stuck-up princess." He looked over at Jenna and added, "No offense."

Jenna flinched, saying ruefully, "We weren't always the nicest."

"But she dropped some names. She said Kim Gordon and John Darnielle were her heroes and she wanted to play like them, and I was like 'Oh, okay, this girl is a lot cooler than I thought.' So I said I'd work with her and we started hanging out. Nothing formal at first, just a couple hours every couple weeks, but then she got more serious about it, and so we started meeting on a regular schedule, like, every Tuesday or whatever."

Max's eyes darted around the room nervously as if someone might stop him at any moment. Though he spoke with a powerful deep bass, there was a shyness about him that was hard to square with the idea of him performing in public.

"When school let out, a lot of her friends were gone for the summer, so we started hanging out more. Mostly just playing — she was getting really good, actually — but we went to a couple shows, and I guess we became friends. But then things got weird."

"Weird how?" Jenna asked.

"Usually she'd just come over to my house — I have a sound-proof garage where we could play as loud as we wanted. But there was this party at her house one night." Max lowered his voice. "She was kind of coming on to me. In front of her brother and all his friends." Jason remembered Jenna's quick dismissal of the possibility that Lacey was into Max: *Max* so *isn't her type*. He looked over, but her face was inscrutable.

"I got the feeling that she was into me, and I was, like, not mad." Jason looked down as Max spoke. Without realizing it, he'd gripped a fork under the table so tightly the blood had gone out of his knuckles. He placed it back on the table and shook out his hand, waiting for Max to continue. "But I had it wrong." He faltered and turned to Jenna. "This is the part I started to tell you."

"Lacey got in a fight with Luke," Jenna offered.

"Is that weird?" Jason asked. *We're close. When he's not being a crazy jock frat boy in training.* If Lacey had described her relationship with her brother that way, maybe they were always fighting.

"It got pretty aggressive. And" — he paused and sipped from his Coke before adding — "she was arguing with Troy, too." Jason's mind went instantly to the snapshot.

"See?" Jenna said under her breath. "It must have something to do with why she left you that photo."

Max looked back and forth between them, and Jason realized he hadn't finished with his story yet.

"So they were mad at her for inviting you?"

"Luke for sure wanted me out of there, and he wasn't shy about saying so. After he made that clear, I didn't really stick around to ask questions. And then after that night, things with Lacey were different. She apologized for her brother, but she stopped texting me so much. Something in her just closed off. She'd check her texts and then look like she'd been swallowed by a dark cloud." He took another long sip of his Coke before continuing. "One day her phone rang, and she said it was Jenna so she had to take it. I wasn't trying to spy on her or anything, but I went out in the driveway to get some air and I could hear her. She was saying all this stuff about secrets and how she couldn't keep lying about them. And then the last thing I heard was 'I'm scared of what Luke will do to us, but I'm more scared of not being with you.'"

"Lacey and I only talked on the phone once that summer, and it was before that night at her house," Jenna said. "Besides, we were close, but not like that." She laughed weakly.

"So Lacey had a secret boyfriend," Jason said slowly. His throat was tight. He knew Lacey had secrets, but he didn't want them to be about another guy. *You have to know that what's between us is real.* He wanted to confront her, but he was scared of what she would tell him. Instead, he asked Jenna, "Who do you think it was?"

She took a minute to think about her answer. "I've been trying to figure this out since you started to tell me yesterday. Don't take this the wrong way, Max, but you're not the first guy who thought he might have had a shot with Lacey. She didn't ever want to tell anybody no."

"Honestly," Max said, "I didn't care who it was. I just didn't want any more drama. I guess she was distracted by everything, because she left her phone at my house."

"And you went through it?"

"*No,*" Max snapped. "I didn't even realize it was there until it rang. I saw a text. It was from someone named Casey, and it said, '911 — I need to see you tonight.'"

"There are two Caseys at Brighton," Jenna said thoughtfully. "Casey Franklin is a freshman, and I'm pretty sure Lacey never even met her. The other Casey was friends with Lacey, but he was also the first boy in our grade to come out, so that doesn't make much sense either." She pressed her lips together. "I guess now we're back to square one. You have to ask her about it. What was the last thing you heard from her?"

"I messaged her that you and I talked. I also asked her . . ." He felt foolish bringing up his mysterious midnight visitor in front of Max. "I asked her about the photo," he finally managed. "And I've mostly stayed off Facebook since then. I'll see if there are any new developments when I get home."

It was only later that night that Jason registered that the girl crying alone in the booth he'd passed on his way out of Michael's had been Camille Piangiani. He wondered idly to himself whether she and Pete had broken up and if so, why. They always seemed so happy together. *The realest thing I have right now.* Lacey's words echoed in his mind. He was beginning to wonder if things were ever what they appeared to be.

CHAPTER 16

At least Rakesh didn't gloat when Jason told him the news about Lacey. "Dude, forget about her. There are plenty of fish in the sea. C'mon, let's find you someone who's not playing mind games with half of Brighton."

"She's not — you're missing the point. Another girl is the last thing on my mind right now," Jason said.

"See, that's your problem."

"Whoever she was seeing has to be part of the reason she disappeared. So what if she had another boyfriend? *I'm* the one she's talking to now. And I said she could trust me."

"Yeah, but you can't trust her." Rakesh's argument was echoing his own concerns, but Jason wouldn't admit it. "She's been lying to you about her past, and mad shady about her present. You don't owe her *anything*, and if I were you, I would get out of this situation yesterday."

"You're not me, though, are you?"

"You're right. If I were you, I would definitely not wear that shirt to school."

Jason looked down at the Ghostbusters logo emblazoned on his chest. He'd gotten the T-shirt at a thrift store in the city, and he liked it, though he hadn't been paying a whole lot of attention when he got dressed that morning.

"What's wrong with my shirt?"

Rakesh sighed dramatically. "Finding you another girl is going to be a nightmare."

"Good, then we can give up on it now," Jason said defiantly.

"If there's nothing I can do to change your mind, then I at least want in on the action. What's our next move?"

"Oh, now you want to be my sidekick?"

Rakesh stared at him indignantly. "A of all, there is a hot girl who faked her own death sending you desperate messages on Facebook. Of course I want a front-row seat to this. B of all, I would never be your sidekick. I am all leading man. But seriously, how are we going to find her?"

Jason had wondered the same thing. "I guess we wait for her next message."

Rakesh rolled his eyes. "Damn, you are not good at this at all. Wait? You want me to wait?"

"I want you to shut up. And if you have a better idea, I am all ears."

Though Rakesh suggested going undercover at Brighton High as British exchange students ("Blimey, mate, did you know a bird called Lacey, eh?" he demonstrated, his accent somewhere between Australian surfer and Russian gangster with a dash of German from a Nazi movie thrown in for good measure), when it came down to it, he didn't have a better idea. And so Jason was left to wait.

He understood Rakesh's impatience. He had spent seventeen years waiting for something to happen, and now that it had, he wasn't thrilled at the prospect of twiddling his thumbs and biding his time until Lacey saw fit to tell him what his next move ought to be. He logged in to his Facebook, and before he could open a new chat with Rakesh, he saw the red "1" in the top left corner of his screen.

My brother has something we need; I need you to get it. He keeps it in the glove compartment of his car. Luckily, there's no alarm, and my dad makes him keep a spare copy of the key taped under the back bumper. But seriously, he will KILL you if he catches you. When you see it, you'll understand why I'm being so intense about this.

One more thing: You have to go TONIGHT. And you have to go alone. No Rakesh. No Jenna. It's the only way we can be sure my secret stays safe.

I hope when this is all over that you'll forgive me for asking so much of you. I don't know what else to do. I've liked you since we started talking, Jason, but I am starting to care about you more than I ever have about anyone, so you have to believe me when I tell you to BE CAREFUL.

Lacey had sent it only a few minutes before, but when he looked at his contact list, there was no green dot next to her name. His heart lurched in disappointment at the sight of it, and for the briefest of seconds, he felt like Gatsby, beating on toward some distant and impossible green light. Then he shuddered. The idea that he and Katie Leigh had something in common was almost as terrifying as the idea of communicating with the dead.

*　　*　　*

Having been mostly rule-abiding since childhood, Jason always thought sneaking out of the house was a question of scaling brick walls and shimmying down tree branches. So when it came time for him to leave under cover of darkness, he dutifully pried open his bedroom window, swung one leg over the sill, looked down the two-story drop, and promptly scrambled back into his room. Why risk breaking every bone in his body when he could exit silently via the kitchen door? Which is exactly what he did. He flinched at the growl of the Subaru's engine when he started the car, but to his good fortune, his mom's room was on the other side of the house than the driveway. He backed out slowly and waited until he'd reached the end of the block before turning on his lights.

After he'd read Lacey's message, he'd gone back to the dusty phone book and entered the Grays' home address into Google maps. He'd checked it on street view to see if he could get a sense of what he'd be up against, but all it showed was a stately Georgian home on an ominously gray day. The sidewalk in front of it was empty, as was the driveway, giving Jason the ghostly impression that it was completely abandoned. If only it were as deserted tonight. It would make his job much easier.

He'd gone around his house with an empty backpack to gather supplies, but after he tossed a flashlight and extra batteries in, he couldn't think of anything he'd need. Breaking into cars wasn't his strong suit, Jason supposed. He'd grabbed a ski mask from his closet, and a crowbar — just in case — and waited for his mom and Mark to go to sleep.

On the drive to Brighton, he tried to picture what he might find in Luke's glove compartment. Alone in his car, he had to keep himself from getting carried away with the gory visions — a severed hand or loose eyeballs like props from a child's birthday party. A gun seemed more likely, though no less alarming.

The house was dark when Jason arrived, and he parked at the end of their street, cutting the engine and calculating his next move. Unlike in the photo he'd seen on Google, there was a silver Mercedes parked in the driveway. Something told Jason that was Mr. or Mrs. Gray's car, not Luke's. Which meant the car he was looking for was out of sight and closer to the house. The lone streetlight was out — a small mercy — and Jason felt like a criminal as he crept up the block, the hood of his sweatshirt pulled up around his face, hands shoved into black jeans. He was about to become a criminal, he supposed, what with the breaking and entering. Or just entering. If he got caught, it probably wouldn't make a difference that he'd had a key. One more reason not to get caught. As if he needed another.

When he reached the Mercedes, he felt under the bumper just in case, but there was nothing there. He made his way up the driveway as stealthily as he could, keeping close to the hedge that ran along the far side. Though the spring air had a wintery bite, nervous sweat beaded on Jason's brow as he approached the back of the house. If any one of the Grays happened to look out a window, they'd surely see him; the only question was how long it would take them to call 911 — or decide to take matters into their own hands.

Behind the house there was a small lot with three cars. One small, the type of practical affair that got good gas mileage, another covered by a tan tarp, and the last a hulking cherry red Jeep. Bingo. He made a beeline and reached under the bumper, glancing behind him to make sure he was alone. There was no one there, but a huge window allowed him to see into the Grays' empty kitchen. He shivered involuntarily. He was about to give up and check the hybrid when his fingers struck something metallic. He tugged at it, and came away with a magnetized case, inside of which was a key. Luke had upgraded his security system since Lacey had last been here. Jason hoped he hadn't added an alarm.

A bass drum seemed to have replaced his heart in his chest, and it pounded away furiously as he slid the key into the passenger-side lock. Part of him hoped it wouldn't turn. He could slink back down the driveway, take himself straight home, and hide under the covers.

He coaxed the door open, the creaking hinges banging like thunder in Jason's ears. The overhead lights popped to life as soon as he did, temporarily exposing him. He winced, and switched the lamp off manually. He was glad he'd had the foresight to bring the flashlight in his backpack, but when its powerful beam nearly blinded him, he cursed himself for losing his pocket-size one in the woods.

Jason didn't know whether to be relieved or disappointed that the glove compartment contained no bloody body parts or weapons. He riffled through the paperwork, wondering if perhaps there was a letter, but it was exactly what you'd expect: insurance, a leather-bound manual, and a few straight receipts. He examined them with the flashlight, but they were from gas stations. Had Lacey sent him on a wild-goose chase? It had been so urgent that he come tonight — maybe Luke had moved whatever Jason wasn't supposed to find. Whoever had texted him seemed to be watching Jason's every move; perhaps they'd gotten here first. Flipping through the pages of the manual, Jason searched for some sort of clue, and when the computer flash drive fell out, he knew he'd found what he'd come for.

"Jackpot," he breathed, feeling for a moment as if he really had won the lottery.

Quickly, he returned everything to its rightful position and locked the car, and he was about to hurry back to the street when he found himself bathed in light. Over his shoulder he saw a man — Mr. Gray, he presumed — clad in a bathrobe and slippers standing in his kitchen with a bewildered expression. At first Jason froze, and then his reflexes sprang into action. He dropped to the ground. If Lacey's dad was coming outside, he'd never get to the bottom of the driveway unseen. He looked around wildly, and decided his best hope for concealing himself was the tarp covering the third car. He army-crawled toward it, and had just ducked underneath when he heard the door open and a man's voice asking, "Is somebody out here?"

Jason was almost certain he'd left everything exactly as he'd found it, but it felt like an eternity before Ed Gray was satisfied enough to return indoors. The door slammed shut, and though the muscles in his thighs were on fire, Jason continued squatting until he was sure the light had gone off as well. He exhaled deeply and straightened his legs. Only then did he become aware of his surroundings.

Under the tarp next to Jason was a boxy black Volkswagen. *I call her Vinnie cause she's vintage.* He flicked on the flashlight to be sure, this time holding his hand over the front to dim it. His breath caught in his throat. It wasn't the physical proximity to something that belonged to Lacey that shook him. It wasn't even the realization that this was definitely the vehicle that nearly ran him down when he was leaving the bridge.

It was the sight of his cowboy-boot flashlight strewn on the backseat that made his blood run cold.

CHAPTER 17

*H*is hands were still trembling when he plugged the USB into his laptop. He'd been so numb on the ride home he hadn't even realized he was shivering. He'd wanted to believe it was Lacey in the car at the bridge, just like he'd wanted to believe it was Lacey in his room the other night. But the threatening messages and the appearance of his flashlight in the car parked at her parents' house, a place she couldn't possibly risk being seen, were making it seem less and less plausible. And if it was Lacey, maybe her intentions weren't as pure as Jason had hoped.

He rubbed his palms together and waited for the drive to appear on his desktop. A video file called "Summer" popped up, and Jason clicked PLAY, terrified of what might appear on-screen. He was sweating again, the cold perspiration coating his body like ice.

The picture was blurry — it looked like nighttime. He turned up the audio as high as it would go as some figures sharpened into focus. The dark sky was illuminated by lanterns and tiki torches. He was looking at a backyard. People were laughing and talking, and Jason could only hear male voices, but at the center of the frame was a girl, her neck down so that her blonde hair covered her face. Her narrow shoulders were shaking and Jason thought she might be crying until she tossed her glossy mane back to reveal a big smile. A familiar smile.

Lacey's smile. Jason gasped, feeling foolish as he heard himself. There was something about seeing her in motion that unsettled him, as if a cartoon ghost had come in through the window and taken the seat next to him. But he was alone in the room and the on-screen Lacey was still making a big show of cracking up. The frame grew wider so that Jason could see Lacey facing someone much taller, stooped over her. He squinted. It was Max. It must have been the party at her house he'd mentioned at Michael's.

"Is that Max Anderson?" The male voice was off camera and Jason didn't recognize it.

"Yup." Another guy. He sounded like he was holding back laughter, and Jason got the sense this was the cameraman.

"What's he doing here?"

"Dunno, but he's been talking to Lacey *alllllll* night."

"Has Luke seen this guy?"

"My guess would be no. Oh *man*, I hope I can be there when he does."

Lacey was bubbly, swatting at Max playfully. The camera captured her as she raised her thin wrists to his chest and pushed him gently. He was more awkward, unaccustomed to the attention. The happy expression on his face didn't look like it got much regular use.

The strange out-of-body feeling Jason had experienced at Michael's came over him again. He was seeing Lacey — his Lacey — for what felt like the first time. How she moved, the way the skin around her eyes crinkled. She was exactly like he'd pictured her. He wanted to protect her, to reach into the screen and into the past and warn her that something terrible was waiting for her on Roxy Choi's balcony. It was agonizing to observe her like this, but he had no choice but to continue watching helplessly.

The Lacey on the screen beamed up at Max, and Jason felt that same knot of jealousy tighten in his stomach. The first boy, the one who sounded angry, muttered something Jason couldn't quite make out as the camera swung around to show a group of athletic guys draped on a cluster of Adirondack chairs on the other side of the yard. Lacrosse players. *They look the same at every school*, he marveled. He could hear strains of Kanye West in the background — their parties were the same, too. As the camera moved, he realized he'd seen this landscape earlier in the night out of the corner of his eye. It was definitely the Grays' house. After a minute, the picture went blank, but there were still seven more minutes left according to the progress bar at the bottom of the player.

When the video resumed, it was quieter, and the lights were much brighter. They were inside, walking down a hallway. There was no one in sight until the camera paused in front of an open door. Through it, he could see Lacey from the side. Freckles dotted her bare arms and the rich cobalt of her top seemed even more saturated against the bright white of her jeans. She was gesturing wildly, and Jason could only pick out snippets of what she was saying. "I can't . . . secrets . . . Luke . . . just a friend." The camera angle shifted slightly and now Jason could see all the way into the room. Troy was standing opposite Lacey with his fists clenched, seething. When he opened his mouth, Jason realized he was the angry spectator from the backyard. "Did you bring him here to make me jealous?"

"Oh, please, as if you're even paying attention." They were both getting louder as they grew angrier, and there was something ugly and hard in Lacey's manner that turned Jason's stomach.

"Shh, do you want people to hear you?"

"I'm starting to think I might. I don't know if I can do this anymore."

"Lacey, think about your brother."

"We could make him understand. Besides, why do you care more about what he thinks than me?" She turned toward the door, and the camera swerved wildly around as Jason realized the cameraman was trying to conceal himself. Whoever was shooting the video sped back down the hallway, taking Jason's view of the unhappy couple along with them. At his computer, Jason threw up his hands in frustration. The scene went black.

When the picture started back up, they were outside once again. The music had gotten louder and the boys were rowdier. There were two circles. In one, Jason recognized Luke, and watched his eyes lock on Max, who was shifting his weight from leg to leg at the edge of the other circle. Luke charged over. He and Max were the same height, but Luke was wider and bulkier by half. He shoved his chest against Max's, and Max stumbled backward but stayed on his feet.

"What are you doing here?" Luke growled.

Max had seemed uncomfortable before, but now he looked utterly panicked. A confrontation with a lacrosse player was more than he'd bargained for. He stepped back and stuttered an apology. Everyone had stopped what they were doing and turned their attention to the budding conflict.

"Seriously, you're not welcome here," Luke spat. At that moment, Troy stepped into the frame, backing Luke up. Luke was obviously enraged, but the fury Jason had seen in Troy's face just a few moments before had disappeared everywhere but his eyes, which flashed with anger. In calm, measured tones he told Max to leave.

Max flushed and started to walk away when Lacey, fists flying, sped across the yard to her brother. Max looked on as they started shouting at each other.

"*I* invited him. He's my friend!"

"He's not your *friend*."

Plenty of people were overprotective of their sisters, but Luke's obsession with Lacey's social circle seemed like a whole other ball game. *Seriously, he will KILL you if he catches you.* Could Luke's lacrosse-fueled rage at the world have crossed over into violence? Was he the reason Lacey had disappeared?

"I'm so sick of you telling me what to do!" Lacey was shouting on-screen.

"You can go," Troy said coldly to Max. "This is a family matter."

"Forget it," Max said quietly, and turned to leave. Instead of stopping him, Lacey swiveled toward Troy and really lost her temper.

"And you! You're not my father, you're not my brother, and you're *not* my boyfriend!"

"Oh snap," came the cameraman's giggle from off screen.

Troy's voice was choked with quiet fury when he answered. "Good. You're a mess, Lacey. I wouldn't date you if you paid me. You deserve to be with someone like Josh Groban over there." He cocked his head and sneered at Max, who paused on his way out of the yard.

Jason wished he could see his face, but all the camera captured was the slightest tensing of his shoulders as he registered the insult. In the background, he could see one of the onlookers' eyes widen. Luke blinked but he didn't avert his gaze from Max as he shook off the Josh Groban comment and then stalked out of the yard. Troy realized he was being filmed and the expression on his face changed from disgust to obvious frustration. "Come on, Sully, turn that off." The picture went dark again, and then ended.

So Troy was the secret boyfriend, and his romance with Lacey wasn't exactly the stuff of fairy tales. But was that enough to make Lacey disappear? Jason dug around his bag for the photo of Troy he'd found on his desk and examined it again. The way they were avoiding eye contact, the secretive meeting, it made more sense now. Troy would have lost his best friend if the news of his and Lacey's relationship had gotten out. Maybe Lacey was right when she'd accused him of caring more about her brother's feelings than her own. Even so, Jason had recovered the video from Luke's possession, so Troy and Lacey's relationship couldn't be a secret to him anymore — and Jason wasn't sure it ever had been.

There were still so many questions. Lacey had said they needed this video, but Jason still didn't understand for what. *I hope when this is all over you'll forgive me.* For having another boyfriend? For following him and threatening him? His patience was beginning to wear thin. He logged in to Facebook, on the off chance she was online, but of course she wasn't.

Instead he reread Lacey's last message to him, and then, before he could change his mind, he opened a new e-mail to Jenna. Lacey had said he couldn't tell Jenna he was going, but now that it was done, he needed help. And after almost getting

caught at her house tonight, he wasn't so keen on blindly following Lacey's instructions anymore anyway.

> I have something to show you. Can I come
> over tomorrow?

Before he pressed SEND he changed "tomorrow" to "today."
It was past three thirty in the morning, and it would be getting
light soon. Maybe things would be clearer then.

CHAPTER 18

Jason would have preferred to go alone. Rakesh had a tendency to steal the spotlight — Jason didn't want the attention for himself, but he had been hoping he and Jenna could focus on Lacey and piecing together what had happened to her. When Rakesh had heard about the video — and everything Jason had gone through to get it — he insisted on tagging along to Brighton. "Maybe I wasn't clear about this," he'd said at lunch, "but when I told you I wanted in on the action, I meant the part where you snuck out of your house and broke into the Brighton lacrosse captain's car." Jason had tried to explain that Lacey had insisted on secrecy, but Rakesh took that as license to question Lacey and her motives further, and the next thing Jason knew, he was inviting Rakesh to join him on the excursion to Brighton that afternoon. "You said Jenna's cute, right?" he asked as they were climbing into the Subaru, and Jason almost kicked him out of the car. But now, as they were sitting in traffic, he wasn't unhappy to have company, even if his company was bouncing along to pop hits on the radio and describing in graphic terms how he'd convince Katy Perry to run away with him if he ever got the chance to meet her.

"She'd never go for it," Jason said when Rakesh had finished.

"Why, because I'm Indian?"

"Yes, Rock," he deadpanned. "Your race is definitely the only reason you could not get a girl."

"Says the white man."

Jason checked his phone. It was fifteen minutes later than he'd told Jenna he'd get to her house, and they were still ten minutes away. He tossed it into Rakesh's lap.

"Can you text Jenna and tell her we're running late. Say '*I'm running late,*' though; she doesn't know you're coming."

"Then she has no idea how happy she'll be when she sees me."

"Seriously, I could make you get out of the car right now and walk all the way home."

"Great, let me just text Jenna that you're in love with her and that you made up a bunch of stuff about Lacey to get close to her before I go." Jason swiped for the phone, but Rakesh pulled it out of reach. "Dude, calm down, I'm telling her we'll be there soon. Why are you getting so worked up about it anyway? You don't like her, do you?"

"No, it's just that I'm thinking about Lacey."

"Ha!"

"Shut up. I know what you're going to say."

"That you should forget about her? That a girl that has a meathead boyfriend already is not worth your time? That she's been totally shady with you? That it's weird that she won't tell you where she is?"

"Yes, that."

"Jason, for real, it's not healthy."

"Look, no one told you to come along, okay?"

"If you can give me one good reason why you care about this person who you never met except on Facebook, or why you trust her even though you know she has been straight up *lying* to you, I'll shut up about it."

"It's hard to explain."

"One good reason. You can't even give me that."

"It's complicated."

"You're going to have to do a little better than giving me your Facebook relationship status."

"She didn't lie to me because she wanted to. Someone made her disappear and now she has to protect herself, and I have to protect her, too. And that involves figuring out what happened, even if I have to deal with some ugly stuff from her past. Or get followed in the woods. Or threatened by who knows who. Someone did this to her, and I promised to help." He left out the way Jenna had looked at him with her saucer eyes; he felt disloyal enough to Lacey for spilling the beans about the contents of Luke's glove compartment as it was.

The only sound in the car was "Tik Tok" blasting from the radio. Normally, Jason would consider the music an affront to his speakers, but he wasn't in the mood to pick that particular battle at the moment. Finally, Rakesh broke the silence. "Ke$ha would definitely go for me."

Jason laughed. "But then you would have to date Ke$ha."

"Who said anything about dating? But now that you mention it, it might be worth it just to piss you off."

"I would literally never talk to you again."

"Like I said: Worth. It."

They pulled up outside the address Jenna had sent them. It was a brick colonial house with green shutters, modest compared to some of the palatial residences on the street, but still significantly nicer than the homes either Jason or Rakesh lived in.

"You didn't tell me she was rich," Rakesh said.

Jason shot him a warning glass. "I didn't know. Don't make a big deal out of it."

When they rang the bell, they could hear the loud old-fashioned chime in the house. Jason half expected a maid in uniform to answer the door. Instead, Jenna greeted them barefoot in black leggings and a gray V-neck T-shirt. A long chain with a purple pendant hung gracefully from her neck.

"This is my friend Rakesh," he explained, after they'd said hello.

Rakesh lifted Jenna's hands to his lips. "My lady," he said formally. "What an impressive abode you have."

Jason glared at him. "Ignore him, please," he said to Jenna, though she was obviously amused.

"Why thank you, good sir," she replied with a curtsy.

"Are your parents here?" asked Jason, eager to put an end to whatever was happening between them.

"My dad's working late," she answered in her normal voice. "And my mom has her book club. So we have my impressive abode all to ourselves. C'mon upstairs. Max is here, too."

The wooden staircase was lined with painted landscapes in ornate frames. "It's like a museum," Jason observed. He thought he heard Rakesh snicker, but he didn't dare look behind him.

"My mom is a lover of culture." Jenna's tone was derisive. "Except when it comes to my iTunes library."

"When did you invite Max?" Jason asked, hoping she couldn't hear the disappointment in his voice. He should be glad — Max had been there when the video was filmed, surely he'd know something about it — but his vision of hunching over the computer with Jenna looking for clues was rapidly turning into a reality featuring a whole Scooby-Doo gang.

"I ran into him in school today, and he asked if you heard from Lacey, so I told him to come over. I hope that's okay."

They were inside her bedroom before he could answer. There was thick beige carpeting and eggshell-colored walls with framed black-and-white photography. Butting out from the opposite side of the generous space sat a double bed with a wildly colorful comforter that stood out against the neutral tones of the rest of the room. Jason had a feeling her mother had "helped" with the decorations, but he got the sense Jenna had chosen the bright centerpiece on her own.

"Have a seat." She swept her hand around the room, and Max looked over his shoulder from her desk. He was scrolling through the aforementioned iTunes library. Jason wondered if The XX playing over the clear computer speakers was his choice or Jenna's.

"I'm Rakesh." He stuck his hand confidently in Max's direction. "Any Rihanna on there?"

Max shook his hand. "Did you know Lacey?" he asked coldly. Jason felt a defensive pang for Rakesh, even though he knew he couldn't care less what Max thought of him or his musical taste.

"Nah, but any girl that gets Jason to commit burglary is a friend of mine."

There was an awkward silence. Jason had told Jenna he had something to show her, but he hadn't explained what or how he'd gotten in. "So I heard from Lacey again last night. She asked me to do something. It's kind of a long story, but it involved taking this." He held up the drive.

"From where?" Jenna asked uneasily.

"Luke's glove compartment." He didn't wait for her to react, pressing on and addressing himself to Max. "It was from the night at her house this summer that you told us about. I mean, at least I think that's what it is. But there's something you didn't see. Do you mind?" He gestured to the computer, and Max stood up.

Jenna and Max and Rakesh gathered around the computer, peering over his shoulder.

"So, um, can we go back to the part where you broke into Luke Gray's car?" Jenna asked, and Rakesh started to tell her about Jason's adventure the night before, but Jason silenced him by playing the video, and he stood up so as not to obscure their view.

Jenna gasped audibly when Lacey threw her hair back. Without thinking, Jason lay a comforting hand on her shoulder, realizing a second too late that he had not escaped Rakesh's hawkish gaze. "Is this the night?" she asked when Max appeared in the frame.

"Yeah." He colored when he heard the partygoers say his name. He muttered something Jason couldn't hear, his eyes trained on the picture. After that, Jason noticed, no one looked away, not even Rakesh. As they watched Lacey's hands settle on Max's chest, Jason felt envy twisting in his gut. He tried to put himself in Troy's shoes. The idea of Lacey with someone else made him feel lonely and empty. And angry, too, if he was being honest with himself. If watching Lacey flirting with Max had sent Troy into a jealous rage, how much further would he need to be pushed to hurt her?

"Holy shnikes," Jenna whispered when Lacey and Troy began fighting.

Realizing they were talking about him, Max's face darkened. "That guy's always been such an ass to me — if this is the reason why, I mean, if it had something to do with what happened to her . . ." he didn't finish the thought, and Jenna glanced over at him sympathetically.

When the camera shifted, Jason asked if they had any idea who was shooting.

"It sounded like John Sullivan at the beginning," Jenna said. "He's on the lacrosse team and he's always got his camera out. It's so annoying . . ." She trailed off as Luke began attacking Max. They watched through the end in silence, and Jenna turned to Max. "God, I'm so sorry."

He looked surprised. "It's not you."

"No, but, like, Luke is my friend. And my other guy friends are always doing stuff like this. I never say anything. It's just that while it's happening it never looks this messed up."

Max shrugged. "Trust me, I'm used to it. And anyway, I'm not the one you need to be worried about. If Troy has it out for Lacey, how long until he figures out she's alive? What if he finds her before we do?"

"I've been wondering the same thing," Jason said. "But also" — he looked nervously at Jenna — "I don't know if we can rule out Luke in all of this. I mean, I got this from his car. So he definitely knew about them. And I am trying not to think about what's gonna happen when Luke figures out this video is gone."

Jenna didn't say anything, but an expression of guilt passed over her face.

"I know he's your friend, but he's been hiding this," Jason added.

"Guys, Luke wouldn't hurt anyone." She didn't sound so convinced. Jason didn't press the matter, but he wasn't, either. He thought back to his Facebook profile. He'd looked mean, pure and simple. Like a bully.

"So what do we do next?" Rakesh asked.

"We?" Max said sharply.

Rakesh didn't bat an eye. "Usually, when someone is missing, you're supposed to report it to the police."

"Lacey told Jason not to do that. But she also told him not to tell you about stealing this video, so I guess all bets are off."

"I've been thinking about this," Jason said, doing his best to ignore Max's sour look. "I don't think we should tell anyone yet. If we go to the police, they'll say we're just kids who've made up a story. Even if they take us seriously, the first people they'd turn to would be Lacey's family. And Luke would probably go straight to Troy, and if he's kept his relationship with Lacey hidden this long, he'll probably figure out a way to keep it hidden longer. We have to keep this to ourselves until we know more about what happened."

"So you think we should just wait until Lacey sends you on another errand?"

"I think we have to do some digging on our own. See if there's anything we can learn about Troy, more about his relationship with Lacey or what he was doing the night she died. Jenna, can you talk to him without giving anything away?"

"I don't know, Luke and I are friends 'cause of Lacey, but I barely know Troy."

"Besides," Max added, "if he's the reason Lacey had to disappear, is sending Jenna to talk to him a good idea? She said so herself, he's dangerous."

145

Jason felt a pang of guilt. "I'm sorry," he told her. "It was a bad idea."

"No, you're right, we need him. We just have to figure out another way in. Maybe I can ask around."

Rakesh threaded his hands together behind his head and leaned back against his seat. "Come on, guys. Have we learned nothing from Sherlock Holmes? Encyclopedia Brown? Nancy Drew? What ever happened to good old-fashioned detective work?"

"You think we should follow him?"

"It's not a bad idea," Jason said. "If we know where he goes, who he sees, what he does, maybe it'll give us some clue about what happened." No one disagreed.

They decided to start the next day. Jenna would do a little stealth research and see if she could learn anything about his schedule, and then Jason would pick her up after school and they would follow him. At first, Rakesh protested that he had a squash meet and they should wait until he was free. But when Max noted he would also have to skip the stakeout due to a rehearsal, Rakesh's complaints suddenly stopped. "Looks like it'll be just the two of you, then," he said suggestively, looking back and forth between Jenna and Jason.

But Jason was thinking about Lacey. Was this what she wanted? He still felt like a blind man feeling around in the dark, but they had all listened to him as if he was carrying a map and a flashlight. All he wanted was to help her, but what if he was only making things worse?

CHAPTER 19

$\mathcal{Y}$ou're out of your mind."

"What? I like this song!"

"This song? *This* one?"

Jenna turned the volume knob so that MGMT's "Kids" blared even louder. "Yes, I love it," she said defiantly and giggled at the look of disgust on Jason's face.

"It's, like, one of the top five overplayed songs in the world. And it wasn't even that good to begin with!"

"Do you have ears? Do you have a *heart*? It's a great song. You can dance to it, but it's serious, too. The reason people are always playing it is it literally never gets old."

"Oh my god. I can't believe I'm on a stakeout with someone who loves 'Kids.' This is what you get when you associate with people who think *The Sunset Tree* is the best Mountain Goats album."

All afternoon it had been like this; Jason had met Jenna at the Brighton High entrance and they had sat in the bleachers observing Troy's lacrosse practice under the guise of watching the JV soccer game taking place on the next field over. They'd waited patiently out of sight next to the field house while Luke and Troy and a few other diehards stayed behind tossing the ball after the official end of practice. At dusk, when Troy left the locker room with Luke, they'd tailed them to the parking lot, and then into town where they'd watched the two guys devour burgers on plates heaped with fries through the glass window of Johnny Rockets. All the while Jason and Jenna had chatted easily like old friends, exchanging stories about school, going back and forth about music, and occasionally mocking one of Troy's jock mannerisms.

"You really don't have a heart," Jenna said.

"*All Hail West Texas* has more heart in a single song than all of *Sunset Tree* combined!"

"I swear, it's like you and Lacey are the same person when it comes to music."

The mention of Lacey's name thudded heavily in their buoyant conversation.

Before the pause grew awkward, though, Jenna pointed into the restaurant. "Look, there's Aaron Majors and Luis Gonzales."

"Friends of yours?"

"No, but they're on the lacrosse team, which means we might be here a while since they tend to travel in a pack."

Luis slid into the booth and Aaron pulled up a chair. A few elaborate high fives were exchanged. Inside the car, Jason rolled his eyes.

"So you're one of those guys who hates high school, huh?"

"And you're one of those girls who loves it?" Jason challenged.

"Yeah, you know, my best friend, who I thought died in a freak accident or was murdered, turns out to be hiding out somewhere and giving me the silent treatment, but other than that it's *peachy*."

Jason was taken aback. Jenna, usually so warm and kind, sounded utterly angry. "I'm sorry," he said softly. "I shouldn't have . . ."

She shook her head. "No, I'm sorry. That wasn't fair. Honestly, before all this stuff happened, I *did* like high school. We'd be in a car seven deep, and I'd be sitting shotgun on Lacey's lap with the radio blasting and the windows down, and we'd be driving to go to some house party, and I'd think, 'This is the stuff people remember.'" She looked at him. "You probably think that's the type of cheesy thing Taylor Swift would sing about. Anyway, now that Lacey's gone, I *do* remember those nights, and I'm even more grateful that we had them, and it makes me want to enjoy what's left of high school. You know, *after* I figure out what really happened to my best friend."

"I'm going to help you do that," Jason said. "And by the way, I love Taylor Swift. A lot. Unironically."

"I knew there was a heart beating somewhere in there." She tapped Jason's chest lightly and smiled the sad smile he'd come to associate with her.

As they watched the boys in Johnny Rockets fumble for their wallets and pool cash on the table, Jason asked Jenna where her parents thought she was.

"Volunteering at an animal shelter. Which I do, but normally the shelter closes at six. What was your excuse?"

"I told my mom I have a chemistry project. It's weird, I think she'd rather I be out partying somewhere than on Facebook."

Jenna rolled her eyes. "Tell me about it. The other day my mom tried to talk to me about sending 'intimate photos.'"

"If my mom ever said 'intimate photos' in front of me, I think I would move in with Rakesh."

"Oh, look, they're leaving." Jenna and Jason shifted their gaze to the diner. On the sidewalk outside, the guys split up — Luis and Aaron heading for one car while Luke and Troy climbed into Luke's Jeep. Jason wondered how he'd reacted when he realized the video had gone missing. Maybe he hadn't noticed yet, though that didn't seem likely considering the urgency from Lacey's instructions. When Luke pulled out of the parking space, Jason waited a minute and did the same, leaving two cars in between them. Brighton was becoming more familiar now that Jason was spending so much time there, but navigating out of town they found themselves on streets Jason had never seen before. He asked Jenna if she knew where they were.

"I think we're going toward Troy's house. He's neighbors with a girl I used to be friends with, and she lives a couple streets over from here. She had the best American Girl doll collection I've ever seen."

"Were you really into American Girl dolls? Is that a phase all girls go through?"

"Yes! Except I was totally obsessed. I had Molly, and I took her with me *everywhere*. Even Lacey made fun of me for it."

"Really?" Jason was incredulous. He was certain Lacey had told him about her own doll, but the night they talked about childhood toys seemed like a lifetime ago now.

Before he could question her further, they watched the SUV slow to a stop, and Jason pulled over halfway down the block. Troy jumped out of the car and grabbed his lacrosse bag from the backseat, slinging it over his shoulder. They waited until they saw Luke's brake lights disappear around a corner before pulling up to Troy's house. A few of the lights were on, but there were no people visible through the windows.

"So now we wait?" Jenna asked.

"I guess so."

Considering how little progress they were making on uncovering Troy's darkest secrets, Jason was in a pretty good mood. If he had met Jenna in school, he would have dismissed her as just another generic popular girl. At first glance, she seemed just like the pretty girls from Roosevelt, the ones who piled into shiny cars on Saturday nights wearing the same designer jeans, the same ruffled tops, the same lip gloss. Rakesh was friends with those girls. Most of them were perfectly nice, some of them were plenty book smart, but all of them were hopelessly boring.

Jenna was a lot of things, but boring wasn't one of them. She was funny and opinionated — even if most of her opinions about music were wrong — and she treated Jason like an honest-to-god interesting person, not just a sidekick who might help her get closer to the most sought-after guy in school. She was telling him about a night when she and Lacey had told their parents they were sleeping at each other's houses, gone to a Feist concert in the city, and then wound up crashing on the dorm room floor of two guys they'd met there after they realized they couldn't go home. He was laughing when he saw the front door to Troy's house open.

"Look," he whispered, as if Troy could hear him from across the street.

Troy had unlocked a station wagon and was climbing into the driver's seat. Jason waited until the taillights reached the end of the block before starting the Subaru. They did their best to stay at least a block behind him, but between the hour and their distance from the center of town, there were fewer cars on the streets; Jason prayed they weren't too conspicuous. Jason asked Jenna if she had any idea where they were headed.

"Could be one of his buddies' houses, but . . ."

"But what?"

At first Jenna didn't answer. And then they hung a left, and she finally said, "The cemetery where Lacey is buried is on this road."

"Oh."

As soon as she said it, Jason knew that was Troy's destination. Night had fallen, and the energy in the car had suddenly grown tense. In the headlights, Jason began to see headstones dotting the fenced-off grass on either side of the road. *The cemetery where Lacey is buried.* Jenna had said it so simply, but it wasn't simple at all. Lacey *wasn't* buried.

"It could be a coincidence," Jason said, but Jenna didn't even bother to reply.

Troy turned sharply into the road leading into the graveyard, but Jason pulled over before the entrance. "I guess I should park here so he doesn't see us." He killed the engine but neither of them moved.

"Do you know where it is? Her grave, I mean."

Jenna nodded. "Not far. I haven't been here since the funeral. It's too depressing. It's why I wanted that memorial." Jenna's voice was strangely flat and disembodied in the dark. "I know this was the whole reason we're following him, but I honestly didn't think he'd do something like this. I kind of don't want to get out of the car."

Jason couldn't see her face, but he realized she was scared. Out of nowhere there was a loud beep and Jason jumped with fright. He heard Jenna fishing around in her bag. "Just my phone," she said with a nervous laugh. The glow from the screen illuminated her face and soothed Jason's jangly nerves.

"It's Max — he wants to know how it's going." She thought for a minute. "We should wait until we know something before we answer."

Their eyes met. "Come on," Jason said, opening his car door. "It'll be fine." He wished he believed it to be true. He took her elbow and guided her up to the entrance to the park. The streetlights from the road dimly lit the path they trudged up, but the farther they got into the cemetery, the deeper the night grew. There was something otherworldly about being in a cemetery at night. Marble monuments shone eerily in the darkness, and the moon cast shadows over the soft grass beneath their feet. In the absence of light, all the flowers Jason could see looked black, as if the petals had been touched by some sinister force and the stems were infected by death. He shivered, hoping Jenna didn't notice.

Jason had been yawning all day, his midnight trip to Brighton catching up to him, but now his body pumped with adrenaline. He could hear their individual footsteps and the soft rhythm of their breathing. He was glad they were both wearing dark clothing that wouldn't stand out if Troy happened to be approaching from the opposite direction.

Jenna led the way without speaking. There was still no sign of the station wagon, and they stayed a good distance from the road, weaving between the neat rows of stone slabs. Finally Jenna stopped and turned to him. "Up there," she whispered. "At the top of the hill, just past those trees." She didn't move, so he began walking up the hill, his curiosity outweighing his fear. A moment later, she was by his side, pointing to Troy's car, which was pulled to the side of the narrow road as if it had been abandoned.

They crept behind the thick trunk of an oak tree, and Jason blinked, waiting for his eyes to adjust. They stood as still as statues, barely breathing. Thinking about the skeletons beneath their feet, Jason felt his skin grow clammy. The idea that one of these plots was Lacey's sickened him. Had he had it wrong all along? Was she underground, lying there lifeless, her ghost responsible for the messages he was receiving? He pushed the thought out of his mind the moment he heard rustlings. It sounded like someone was being strangled, and he wrapped his hand protectively around Jenna's wrist. With her free hand, she covered her mouth in horror. She had seen something he hadn't, and he followed her gaze until he could make out Troy's silhouette as he kneeled on the ground.

Just then, a cloud that had been covering the moon passed, and a beam of light caused Jenna's and Jason's shadows to stretch out along the tidy row of headstones right up to Troy's back. But Troy didn't notice, and it was at that moment that Jason realized the choking noise was the sound of Troy weeping. Blood rushed into Jason's ears, and he caught his breath.

"I'm sorry, I'm sorry, I'm sorry," Troy sobbed quietly, repeating the words over and over again. In the moonlight, Jason could see him digging at the earth with his fingernails, occasionally lifting one hand to wipe his face. "I'm so sorry, Lacey." Jenna gasped, and Troy looked up. "Who's there?" he called into the shadows.

They stood frozen in place, so near each other Jason could smell the clean scent of Jenna's shampoo, and Jason's heart was pounding so loudly he feared Troy would be able to hear it. To Jason's great relief, he remained on his knees at the base of the cold gray headstone, though the crying grew softer until finally it subsided entirely. Troy sat a moment longer, and finally got up to go. Jason and Jenna ducked to the other side of the tree as they waited for him to pass. After what felt like an eternity, they heard his car start and watched as his taillights faded down the road. Jason began to approach the plot, but she grabbed his wrist and pulled him back.

"I want to get out of here." If he hadn't been standing a few inches from her, he wouldn't have heard, but the urgency came through loud and clear. He desperately wanted to know what Troy had been doing, but he wasn't too keen on sticking around the moonlit graveyard much longer, either. So he cautiously led Jenna back along the path to the street.

Jenna's hands were shaking as she pulled at the door to the Subaru. Jason helped her inside. "My curfew," she said when he started the car. It was 9:57. As if they didn't have enough to be worried about.

"I can get you home in five minutes," he said reassuringly. His mind was still with Troy. "Am I making this up or did we just see Troy Palmer sobbing?"

"Unless we were having the same hallucination, that is what we just saw."

"Do you think he was saying sorry because . . ." The words hung in the air.

"I don't know," Jenna said. Neither said what they each knew the other was thinking.

"What was he doing to the ground?"

"He was burying something."

"What? How do you know that?"

"I saw something gold catch the light. Do you think he knew we were there?"

"I think he would have done something if he knew." *Like kill us*, Jason added to himself. "We have to find out what he buried."

"Left here," she interrupted. "There, that's my house up there."

She hopped out of the car. "We'll talk tomorrow," she said tightly. He couldn't tell if her worries stemmed from fear of Troy or anxiety about her curfew. He wanted to tell her it would be okay, but there was no time. Besides, just like earlier, he wasn't sure whether or not he believed it.

CHAPTER 20

t first, Jason headed toward Oakdale. Over five thousand songs on his iPod, and not a single one capable of calming him down. His fingers twitched on the steering wheel, and he called Rakesh on speaker phone. It rang through to voice mail.

"Hey, just wanted to tell you about my night. Pretty ordinary stuff, like, I saw the cocaptain of the Brighton lacrosse team crying in a graveyard. He buried something. In a totally normal way. Okay, call me back."

At a red light, he logged in to Facebook. The message from Lacey was only two words.

Look deeper.

Jason felt sick when he read the words. He'd wanted her to finally explain what was going on, but here were more instructions. And they were cryptic — as usual — but Jason still knew exactly what they meant. He had to go back to the graveyard. Alone.

In the back of his mind, he'd been thinking about his bed waiting for him. As edgy and tense as he was, the idea of his soft inviting mattress, the plush down comforter, the fluffy pillows — his bed was calling to him like a siren. But he'd already turned the car around, was already five minutes from the entrance to the cemetery. How had Lacey known he'd been there? How did she know what he'd missed?

This time he drove through the open gates and down the half mile of road he and Jenna had followed on foot. A squirrel dashed in front of his car, and Jason slammed on his brakes, stopping just before he hit it. His heart was hammering in his chest, and he half expected to see zombies rising out of the earth. He accelerated again until the oak trees he'd concealed himself in earlier were in sight, and then he cut the engine and switched off the headlights.

A chilling breeze had kicked up, it had cleared the sky of the cloud cover, allowing the moon to shine bright and cold overhead. It was almost full, illuminating the stray, gray puffs of cloud that lingered. It was the type of night that was made for a witch on a broomstick. Or digging up something that didn't belong to you at the grave of someone you doubted was dead. Jason might have preferred the witch, not that anyone had given him a choice.

Jason's limbs felt like sandbags. The closer he got to the grave, the less he wanted to see it. He kept reminding himself Lacey wasn't underneath, but it didn't help. He squinted through his glasses, trying to make out the names carved onto the headstones.

Beloved Father, Brother, and Husband: James Keegan.
Martha Nolan, who lives on in our hearts.
Shane Ryan, friend to all he met, loved by all who knew him.

He wondered, if he were to die here, tonight, what would his say?

Jason Moreland, loner.

He shook the thought from his head. Some of the

engravings were too worn down to read. Instinctively, he reached for the flashlight on his key chain, and then remembered that the last time he saw it, it was locked in Lacey's car. A new wave of fear crashed over him, but it was tinged with something else: hope. Maybe she'd summoned him here to finally reveal herself. Before the idea took him any further, he spotted her gravestone and froze.

Dark marble rose elegantly from the grass, and Lacey's name arched boldly across the top, the dates marking her birth and her death below. He swallowed, and his throat felt like it was coated in chalk. It wasn't the idea of Lacey being dead that upset him — that idea was plenty creepy, but by now he was almost used to it — it was the headstone. It was so . . . lifeless. At the memorial, you could feel Lacey's presence; the space was filled with love for her. In contrast, the cemetery felt like a sea of abandonment. People left behind by the ones they'd cared about most, memories buried to rot, bodies deserted by their souls. Jason's whole self buzzed with fear, and he switched into high gear. The sooner he did what he came to do, the sooner he could get out of this haunted field.

He dropped to his knees where Troy had left the spongy earth loose and sank his fingers into the dirt, pulling up tufts of grass as he went. The earth had been softened by the spring rains, and the soil came away easily. Jason unsuccessfully tried to block out the fact that the ground he was digging into was literally littered with bodies. His fingers had just brushed something hard and metallic when he was overcome with the sensation that he was not alone. His neck jerked up, and he swiveled his head.

"Who's there?" he cried softly, and only when the words were out of his mouth did he realize he was going through the exact same motions Troy had earlier. He released the item he'd discovered in order to turn toward the oak tree he'd hidden behind with Jenna, but no one was there. He scanned the rest of the cemetery, half expecting to see the clown from *Hamlet* leading Ophelia's funeral procession. As far as he could tell, he was completely alone. So why did he feel so shaken?

Returning to the small hole he'd created, he sifted through the dirt until he found the object he'd stumbled on. It was a delicate, thin chain with a flat pendant hanging from it. This must have been the gold Jenna had seen in the light. Jason pushed his glasses up his nose; her vision must be a lot better than his. Dangling the necklace from his fingertips, Jason felt the sides for hinges; maybe it was a locket with a clue inside. Instead, his fingers fumbled over an engraving. He wiped away the remaining dirt, and shifted the face into the moonlight to read what it said.

LG + TP

KC

Just then, a shriek ripped through the night, and Jason leapt to his feet, his eyes widening in terror before he identified the interruption as the sound of his phone's ringer. He reached into his pocket, but his hands were shaking so much he couldn't answer until the third ring.

"Hello?" he whispered.

"Dude, it's like you *want* me to miss all the good stuff."

"Rakesh, I can't talk right now."

"Why are you whispering? I know your mom and Mark can't hear you from their room."

"I'm not at my house."

"Where are you, then?" Rakesh demanded. There was a

pause while Jason cradled the phone on his shoulder and held the necklace up to his face so he could examine it. "Wait, are you at Jenna's? Bow chicka bow bow!"

"I'm not at Jenna's," he hissed, blushing at Rakesh's suggestion there was something more than friendship going on between them. "I'm at the cemetery. Troy buried something, and I came back to get it."

"You're digging up something from a graveyard? Have you never seen a horror movie in your life? You have to get out of there. Also, seriously, since when did you become the guy who sneaks around Brighton breaking into cars and stealing things from grave sites?"

"I'm not stealing anything," Jason answered, still distracted by the necklace he was holding. "What do you think KC is?" As soon as he said it, he realized the connection.

"What are you talking about?"

"KC," Jason repeated, his voice rising with excitement. "Casey. It's got to have something to do with the phone calls she was getting."

"Jason, I'm worried about you. You're in a freaking cemetery alone at midnight digging up graves and babbling about someone named Casey. Do I need to come get you? I'm pretty sure I can steal my dad's car."

"Even if you could get halfway out of the driveway before your dad murdered you, what would you do then? You don't even know how to drive!"

"So you *do* want me to come rescue you?"

"No, I'm fine, I'm about to . . ." Behind him, Jason heard rustling. The tension that had been slowly easing out of his shoulders as he settled into the familiar conversation with

Rakesh returned with a vengeance. He felt like every hair on his body was standing at attention.

"Look, I gotta go," he said slowly into the phone, dropping his voice to a whisper.

"What's happening? Are you okay?"

Jason turned around, finding only emptiness. The branches of the oak tree were swaying in the breeze, but he was certain the noise he'd heard had come from much closer. He hadn't realized how many person-size monuments there were for someone to crouch behind. To his left he saw the pit of a grave that been freshly dug. Somehow he'd missed it earlier, and it sent shivers coursing down his spine to think about a coffin being lowered into it. Rakesh was right; he had to get out of there.

"Jason? I'm calling the police," Rakesh was saying.

"No, don't," he protested. "I have to go. I'll call you back."

"Okay, but if I don't hear from you in ten minutes . . ." Jason ended the call before Rakesh could finish the threat.

Jason slipped the necklace into his pocket and started toward the Subaru, but something was stopping him. He turned back toward Lacey's grave, and this time instead of seeing Ophelia's funeral, he pictured Lacey's ghost wandering among the grassy rows. The necklace weighed like lead in his pocket. He didn't believe in curses or anything like that, but Rakesh's warning about removing items from the resting place of the dead rang in his ears, and he knew he had to leave it behind. He hastily removed it and dropped it back in the small hole he'd created. Using the tip of his sneaker to fill in the rest of the dirt and the clumps of grass, he looked around him one last time, and, satisfied he was free of evil spirits, walked as quickly as he could back to his car.

CHAPTER 21

When Jason walked through the front door, he found his mom reclining on the sofa with a book on her lap, her eyes half shut.

"Hiya, sweet pea." She yawned. "Where ya been?"

"The chemistry project," he reminded her. "Lacey lives out toward Brighton." *Six feet* under *Brighton*, he added silently in his head, *if you believe her headstone, which I don't.*

She looked at her watch. "It's almost one in the morning. They're gonna put you in child services if they find out I let you stay out this late to do homework. We should both go to sleep. Mark's probably up there, snoring away."

"Yeah." He feigned exhaustion even though his heart was still racing. "I'm beat."

She rested a hand lightly on his back. "Have you been doing okay lately, kiddo? Some days, I swear, it's like you've got the weight of your world on your shoulders. I don't mean to pry about Lacey, but you'd tell me if something was going on, right?"

What would she do if he told her the truth — that there *was* something going on but he couldn't talk about it because everyone thought she was dead? That a psycho lacrosse player had scared her or hurt her enough to allow them to think that? His mom would take away his laptop for life, that much he knew; what was up for grabs was whether it would happen before or after she locked him in a mental institution.

"I'm fine, Mom. And there's *nothing* going on with Lacey — I'm just a little stressed about the chemistry project. I want to do well on it."

She frowned. "Your grades are important to me, but sometimes I wish you'd worry less about school. You're a smart kid, the project will be fine. You should loosen up sometimes. Grades aren't everything."

"I'll remind you of that the next time you see my report card."

"I mean it, Jason. As your mother, I can say with authority that your happiness is more important to me than straight As. You have the best heart of anyone I know; you should let people see it occasionally." Involuntarily, he thought of Jenna. *So there is a heart beating in there somewhere.* He fought back a grin, and then felt a pang of guilt. Lacey was the one who was supposed to make him smile like that.

"Thanks, Mom," he mumbled. "Seriously. You don't have to worry about me. I'm going to go to bed now, okay? I love you."

"Sleep well." She hugged him tightly. They headed upstairs together. "Oh, and have a good weekend." When he looked at her blankly, she laughed. "You totally forgot, didn't you? Mark and I are going to his sister's lake house for the weekend. I was sure you and Rakesh were planning some sort of party. You really *are* a good kid. I'll leave cash for pizza and emergencies by the phone in the kitchen. Don't make me regret anything I said to you tonight."

He smiled weakly and shrugged. Under other circumstances he probably would have hosted a rager. As it was, he was just happy he wouldn't have to explain his comings and goings.

Something told him he'd be back in Brighton before the weekend was over.

As soon as she had shut the door to her room, he logged on to his computer. After he'd gotten off the phone with Rakesh, he'd spent the entire car ride home composing the message in his head; it tumbled off his fingertips and onto the screen.

L,

It feels weird writing this. I get the strangest sense you already know everything I'm going to say. But maybe I'm imagining things. Feels like I'm doing a lot of that lately. Anyway, here goes . . .

I did what you asked. I went back to your grave (literally can't even believe I'm typing this stuff). If you don't know this part, me and Jenna followed Troy (Dick Tracy style), and when it got dark out, he drove to the cemetery. If you told me this morning I was going to see the cocaptain of the Brighton lacrosse team crying like a baby, I'd have said you were a liar, but if you told me six months ago I'd be e-mailing with someone everyone thought was dead, I wouldn't have believed that, either, so maybe I just need to work on my powers of imagination.

Anyway, it was pretty intense, and it freaked Jenna out enough that she wanted to get out of there. So I took her home, but after I got your message, I went back. Which is what you wanted, right? I hope so, cause it wasn't exactly fun being in a graveyard in the middle of the night. But I did find your necklace. Troy buried it there when he was bawling his eyes out and telling you he was so sorry.

I'm starting to piece together what happened to you, but I know there are things you're not telling me. Is it because you were dating Troy? I'm not gonna pretend I love the idea of that, but you still don't have to hide it from me. I care about you. And if he hurt you, if he's the reason you had to disappear, I'll...I don't want to finish that sentence, but Lacey, you should know I would do ANYTHING to protect you.

Anyway, I guess that's it for now. I hope this isn't weird to say, but I miss when things between us were easy. Sometimes I think if you would just see me, face-to-face, we could figure this out. But I understand it's complicated. Just remember, I am here for you.

— J

After he hit SEND, the exhaustion hit him like a ton of bricks. He crawled into bed, and was surprised to find that he was almost *happy*. Yes, there was a lot about Lacey that he didn't understand. But even though his mind was swimming in uncertainty, there was something satisfying about it. Jason had spent more nights than he could count lying in bed, combing over every horribly boring detail of his day, and as bizarre as everything was, he was grateful to finally have real things to think about. Besides, he was on the verge of learning what had happened to Lacey. When he found the obituary and his perfect girlfriend turned into a ghost before his eyes, he'd felt like he'd been stripped of something, but that thing she'd given him originally — the sense of mattering — was gradually coming back to him. Despite everything, he was enveloped by a deep sense of peace and fell asleep with the rock-solid knowledge that everything was going to be okay. In retrospect, he realized, that should have been his first sign that something was wrong.

Bleary-eyed, Jason checked Facebook on his phone as he idled outside Rakesh's house. He'd overslept, and his brain still felt thick with slumber. He tried to ward off his disappointment that Lacey hadn't answered his message. He told himself even runaway missing girls had to sleep sometime.

Rakesh was already grumbling when he climbed into the passenger seat. "Where's my breakfast?"

"Shut up, Rakesh."

"I want an Egg McMuffin! I thought I told you to bring me breakfast." When Jason had called him from the car the night before, Rakesh had demanded he be brought a breakfast sandwich as payback for, as he put it, "missing the good stuff." As with most of his friend's requests, Jason ignored it.

"Can you at least wait until I get a cup of coffee in me before you start complaining?" Jason backed out of the driveway. Rakesh kept his mouth shut. Until they were halfway to Roosevelt High, that is.

"Yo, where are we going?" he asked.

"Um, school?" Jason answered, confused. It was Friday. They were already running late for homeroom.

"No, no, no. We're not going to class right now."

"What are you talking about?"

"We have to go get that necklace."

"You're the one who told me to leave it there last night!"

"Yes. It was midnight. You can't take something from a cemetery at midnight." Rakesh spoke slowly, as if Jason was stupid. It didn't help that Jason stared at him blankly. "But now the sun is shining. Nothing bad can happen. We have to go back and get it. It could be evidence."

"Evidence of what?" Even though daylight was a lot less frightening than the darkness, Jason still wasn't keen on making a third trip to the cemetery.

"Who knows, but don't you think Lacey wants you to get it?"

Invoking her name had the intended effect. Jason sped past the Roosevelt parking lot and steered the car toward Brighton.

It had turned into a beautiful morning by the time they arrived at the cemetery. Rakesh may have entirely made up the rules about when you were and were not allowed to remove items buried at grave sites, but it was definitely less spooky during the day. All the same, it still weirded Jason out to think about the rows and rows of bodies buried around them.

"So you rolled up here *alone* last night?" Rakesh asked when they got out of the car. The respect in his voice was a peace offering, and Jason accepted it with a nod. He didn't want to be fed up anymore, and Rakesh was at least trying to help. Jason pointed out the tall trees where he and Jenna had hidden. In daylight, he could see the tips of their branches were dotted with the first tiny pale green sprouts of spring leaves. It was strange and also comforting to think about something blooming here among the dead.

When they arrived at Lacey's small plot, it was like Rakesh could read Jason's mind. "I wonder what's buried here."

"Dunno," Jason said. "Maybe an empty coffin. Maybe someone else."

Rakesh shivered dramatically. "So creepy." He nudged a clump of loose grass with his toe and asked, "What now?"

"We dig, I guess," Jason answered, though he was unsure. It was true that the space seemed less haunted by the light of day, but the sun posed other problems: Like a passerby seeing two teenagers digging something up in a graveyard and jumping to conclusions. Jason didn't even want to imagine how a security guard would react when he explained it was okay because there was no one buried there.

He hadn't done as well as he thought covering his tracks from the night before. Half the grass was uprooted and the dark base of the headstone was covered in dirt. He dropped to his knees. Rakesh knelt next to him. Troy's and Jason's previous forays made the soil easy to sift through, and it didn't take long for Jason and Rakesh to assemble a small pile next to a neat hole. And then the hole grew wider. And deeper. A rock formed in Jason's stomach. The necklace wasn't there. He sat back on his heels and after a moment Rakesh did, too, knowing better than to say anything.

"I swear, it was here last night. I left it here last night."

They both peered down into the pit that had formed, and Jason felt around the edges in case he had missed something, but he was just going through the motions. Someone had taken the necklace. He was certain of it.

Just then, Jason felt a throbbing ache in his side, his glasses went flying, and all of a sudden he was on his back with the wind knocked out of him. He patted at the ground, fumbling in vain for balance.

"What the . . ." he heard Rakesh from next to him, but his blurry vision was filled with Luke Gray's face, staring down at him in fury.

CHAPTER 22

Jason watched as Luke issued a swift kick to Rakesh's gut, and Rakesh curled up on the ground, his face contorted in pain. Neither could speak or move as Luke bent over them and wrapped a hand around Jason's throat, pinning him down.

"Who are you?" He pushed down on Jason's neck. Hard. "Why are you digging up my sister's grave?" he bellowed. Jason's eyes rolled back in his head as he struggled to breathe.

"Can't we all just get along?" Rakesh wheezed, and Luke momentarily released his hold on Jason's windpipe to kick Rakesh in the stomach again, this time rendering him silent, save for a groan.

"I'm talking to your friend," Luke said, resuming his choke hold on Jason. Up close his skin was smooth and his features were almost childlike, but years of beating other guys with a lacrosse stick had conditioned him to twist his boyish face into menacing expressions of cruelty. He rested a knee on Jason's chest, and Jason hoped desperately the passerby he'd dreaded being caught by would come to his rescue. "I asked you, what are you doing here?"

Jason was still trying to draw breath into his lungs when he was blinded by Luke's fist smashing into his eye socket. He'd never been punched in the face before. It hurt. A lot. It felt like fireworks were exploding in his skull. He tried to muster the strength for a response before Luke could hit him again.

"What do you want from my sister?" Luke shoved him deeper into the dirt.

If he didn't break free, Luke was going to pummel him until he was dead, he was sure of it. He pulled his wrist back to swing again. "Answer me!"

"Friend," Jason gasped. "I'm a friend."

"Why are you digging up the past? Why can't you let her stay buried?" There was something wild in his voice, like he would do anything. *Look deeper.* Had Jason had it all wrong? Was Luke the killer?

"It's not what you think," Jason managed hoarsely.

The next thing he knew, the pressure was gone from his chest, and Rakesh, doubled over from the effort of pulling Luke away, stood above him. Luke sprinted away. "This isn't over," he shouted over his shoulder. "If I see you again, you're a dead man."

Jason wobbled unsteadily to his feet. He blinked back the flashing lights, and a wave of nausea crashed over him. He stumbled a few paces away and spat, blood-tinted saliva dripping onto the well-manicured grass. The pink color was making him woozy, and he dropped to the ground, lying on his back as the sky spun above him. When he tilted his head, he saw Rakesh lying a few feet away. For a moment, there was no other sound than their chests rising and falling.

Jason spoke first. "What just happened?" Talking hurt worse than he'd predicted.

"You just got your butt kicked by a psycho lacrosse player in a cemetery. Well, we both did, but yours got kicked worse. You're welcome for saving your life, by the way."

"Thanks," Jason said. He thought his head might split open.

After a minute, Rakesh helped him to his feet.

"Come on, we have to get out of here in case he calls the cops or something."

Jason nodded, hoping the feeling that he was going to vomit would pass when he started moving. He spotted his glasses; by some miracle, they were neither broken nor bent.

They both limped back to the Subaru, brushing the dirt and grass from their clothes and straightening their hair. When they got to the road, an elderly woman with a bouquet looked at them askance, and Jason wondered just how disheveled Luke had left them. His plaid shirt was caked in dust, and clumps of moist dirt clung to his jeans. Above the neck, Rakesh could have flaunted his perfect bone structure and wavy hair in a shampoo commercial, but his white T-shirt was streaked and torn. When they arrived at the car, Jason saw the purplish hues of a bruise beginning to bloom around his eye in his reflection in the car window.

Rakesh caught him checking himself out. "Looking good," he said sarcastically. "When you're done admiring your battle scars, can you get me out of this god-awful town?"

They didn't even discuss going to school, instead agreeing to go straight to Michael's. As the searing pain in his skull subsided, Jason's mind drifted to the necklace — where had it gone?

"Dude, forget about the necklace," Rakesh said when he voiced his concern. "Can we talk about why Luke Gray wants to kill us?"

"Well, I don't think it helps that we were digging up his sister's grave. I mean, obviously we weren't, but, you know."

Talking hurt more than Jason wanted it to. Thinking did, too, for that matter.

The waitress barely raised an eyebrow at the two hobbling teenagers who arrived just before the lunch rush. She seated them at a comfy booth in the back room, and they took turns going to the men's room to get cleaned up. While Rakesh was gone, Jason sipped at his water, hoping it would help to revive him. He felt like crap.

As soon as he returned, the waitress came by to take their orders. After she was out of earshot, Rakesh asked Jason what he was going to tell his parents about his face.

"Is it bad?" Jason touched the pads of his fingertips to the crease next to his eyelid. Even with next to no pressure, he winced in pain.

"Uh, yeah, you should go look at yourself in the mirror."

Standing up, his body felt creaky and sore. His blood had pumped with adrenaline during the attack, but his energy was waning. The clock above the cash register said it was 11:15 in the morning, which seemed impossibly early with all that had happened since he'd woken up a few hours before. In the bathroom he surveyed himself in the mirror. It was like someone had spread the skin of an eggplant around his eye, attaching it to his face with silver eye makeup. The color was oddly beautiful, and Jason would have marveled at it for much longer if one of the line cooks had not entered the men's room and caught him. He nodded curtly, rinsed his face with cold water, straightened his hair, and headed back to the table.

"So seriously, what story are you going to give Karen?"

"My mom and Mark are going away this weekend."

"What?! Why aren't we having a party?"

"Because we're trying to figure out what happened to Lacey."

"That doesn't mean we can't have a party."

"I'm not having a party. The point is, I have until Monday to come up with a story."

"Why don't I invite some people over to your place tonight, and they can help you come up with a decent cover."

"Don't you get it? Sooner or later my mom is going to catch on to the fact that I have not been disappearing to work on some chemistry project, and when she does, I am not going to be able to get within five feet of my laptop without her looking over my shoulder. I need to find out the truth, and I need to do it *now*."

"So what's your plan for your open house? Are you just going to sit around with Jenna and Max and talk the possibilities to death? Challenge Luke Gray to a duel? Accuse Troy of attempted murder? I probably have internal bleeding from what your precious Lacey's mental case of a brother just did to me, we've made no progress, and all I'm asking is that we have a little fun while we play mission impossible."

Ironic that it was the exact same thing his mother had told him the night before — especially since he was fairly certain his mom would be horrified at the idea of opening up her own house to half of Roosevelt High. He thought of Jenna, too, accusing him of looking down on kids who had a good time. But how was he supposed to enjoy himself like a normal teenager when Lacey would never enjoy herself again? That was the part no one could explain to him. Everybody was so convinced high school was this big party, but if that was the case, then Jason was pretty sure his invitation had been lost in the mail.

He glowered angrily at Rakesh, but Rakesh ignored him. "You could invite Jenna," he said in a singsong.

"Oh, god." Jenna. Last night it had been so easy to talk to her, but now, between his own lack of clarity and her loyalty to Luke, the idea of explaining what had happened seemed too daunting. The only thing that didn't seem too daunting was crawling into bed and pulling the covers over his head. His cheekbones were throbbing and his insides felt like they'd had a few whirls in a salad spinner, and he knew he'd have to make an appearance at school this afternoon unless he wanted to risk someone in the office calling his house to check up on him.

"No one's coming to my house until I figure out what happened to Lacey," he said as firmly as he could. "We're close. I can feel it."

"Pretty sure the only thing you're feeling is the aftereffects of Luke's fist in your face," Rakesh grumbled before letting the subject of the party drop.

CHAPTER 23

It didn't hurt when he didn't touch it. It took Jason a little while to get it through his head; every time he caught his reflection, his fingers immediately went to the dark and shiny swollen skin around his left eye. And each time, he would wince, and then adjust his glasses, which only made the pain worse. He'd tried putting in his contacts, but his eyelid was too misshapen. He made every effort to stop checking himself out, but the only upside to the beating he'd taken was that he was kind of into what the bruise was doing for his face.

He'd fallen asleep in front of the TV, and woken up in the middle of the night to find his eye socket throbbing, his torso sore. Bathed in the strange blue glow of the television screen, he fumbled for the lamp, and then blinked rapidly against the harsh light. His eyelashes were like anvils against his cheeks, sending searing pains shooting through his head. When his sight had adjusted, he hunted for his phone in the couch cushions. No missed calls. After he'd left school, there'd been nothing more from the anonymous number. His text to Jenna had been simple, suggesting they meet up the next day, and she'd agreed. He'd wanted to write Lacey, but he couldn't figure out what to say. Still, on a whim he checked Facebook to see if she had written him.

She had.

Maybe it was the fact that he was awake in the early hours of the morning for the third night that week. Maybe it was the soreness he felt all over. Maybe it was just good old-fashioned intuition. Whatever it was, something told Jason he didn't want to see the message. So he sat disoriented on the couch for a few more minutes. Jason had woken up in the middle of the night feeling unsettled plenty of times before, like his whole existence was off-kilter or the wrong shape, but Lacey had changed that. Or at least he'd thought she had. She had righted him, made him feel like he fit. But now everything hurt — literally — and nothing made sense. The day before, he'd been so full of hope, but now, after another confusing series of events, he wondered if he was further from the truth than he had been when he started.

When he'd first discovered the obituary, he'd thought maybe he could walk away. Yes, Lacey was the best thing that ever happened to him, but maybe she wasn't worth all of the trouble. And then he'd gambled, something he didn't do terribly often and didn't have too much experience with. He'd decided she was worth a whole world of trouble, and he bet on her. And now he was scared he'd lost, but it was too late to walk away from the table.

So even though dread had gathered into a pit in his stomach, he opened Lacey's message. And his insides lurched when he saw what she had sent. It was a photo of her. Her lips were curled into a coy smile, and her eyes were turned upward to the camera, as if she were batting her eyelashes just for Jason. In the background, he could see the narrow buds of leaves coiled up, waiting to bloom. The photo was taken on a beautiful spring day. Like today had been. And between Lacey's fingers, she held a familiar delicate gold chain.

`Come and find me`, her message read.

Using his thumb and forefinger, he enlarged the photo as much as he could. There was no question about it. She was wearing the necklace.

Jason was supposed to be overjoyed. Finally, after all of his waiting, here was the long-sought-after invitation to meet. Lacey was alive and well. She was *happy*. So why did he feel queasy and hollow, as if he'd gobbled up bags and bags of month-old Halloween candy and was dealing with the aftereffects?

The problem was that Lacey was playing games. Sending him to a cemetery in the middle of the night, only to reclaim the item he'd been chasing. Directing him to her parents' house so she could show off the prize she'd stolen from him. It was like she was taunting him. He'd fallen for Lacey because she was so straightforward and honest, and now that person was splitting open at the seams, and it scared Jason more than any of his midnight forays to Brighton had.

He stared down at the photo. She was so beautiful. *Come and find me*. The picture had been taken outside. The tree behind her was about to blossom, but that narrowed it down to just about every tree Jason had seen in the last week. In addition to the necklace, Lacey was wearing a purple T-shirt, which didn't seem out of the ordinary. There had to be some sort of clue he was missing, but he was too tired to see it. The clock read 3:42. There was nothing he was going to be able to do about it now. He would ask Jenna if she had any idea where it was taken — or who it was taken by — tomorrow.

Wearily, he turned off the light and dragged himself upstairs and into bed. When he lowered his heavy eyelids, the fatigue overtook his anxiety, and the next thing he knew, the sun was streaming into his bedroom and it was close to noon on Saturday morning.

The bruises were still fresh and sore, and his rib cage ached as he fastened his seat belt across it, but the night of sleep had been good for his spirits. Lacey's mysterious message seemed less sinister now — she was only trying to protect herself — and she was within reach. Jenna was going to help him find her. Jason was loath to admit it, but he was looking forward to Jenna's reaction to his battle wounds.

When he arrived at her front door, he was not disappointed. Concern took over her face and she hugged him tightly before asking, "Oh my god, Jason, what *happened*?"

He looked around nervously for her mother. As cool as he thought he looked, meeting someone else's parents with a black eye couldn't be a good idea. As if thinking the same thing, she quickly added, "Come on, let's go up to my room."

Once he was seated on her bed, Jason started where they'd left off together: with him dropping her off on Thursday night.

"I was on my way home. I mean, you were in that cemetery with me, it was not the type of place anyone sane would go sneaking around in alone at night. But then Lacey messaged me."

Jenna was scrolling through her iPod for music; at the mention of Lacey's message, Jason watched her shoulders tense. "What did she say?"

"'Look deeper,'" Jason said. "I don't know how she knew what we'd seen, but I went back. And you were right. Troy *did* bury something. He left a necklace there. It was engraved with their initials, and the letters *K* and *C*."

"*K* and *C*? What does that mean?"

"I'm not sure, but when you say it, it's KC. Casey. Like the call Max saw her get."

"Can I see the necklace?" She had put on Fleetwood Max's *Rumours*, and now her attention was fully on Jason.

"Well, you can't take something . . ." At first he started to repeat Rakesh's arbitrary rules for removing objects from cemeteries, and then thought better of it. "I left it there. And I even went back for it, because I thought it might be evidence or whatever. But it was gone."

"Gone?"

"Yeah. Totally gone. But then, I got this." He handed over his phone, and Jenna gasped, covering her mouth in shock.

"Who sent this to you?" she demanded.

"Lacey," Jason answered. He thought it was obvious. "Look at the blue sky — the flowers. It has to have been taken recently. Like, yesterday. Do you have any idea where?"

She shook her head. "It's so small on the phone. I'd need to see it on a bigger screen. But wait, what happened to your face?"

"Oh, right." He sheepishly explained about how Luke had caught him and Rakesh back at Lacey's grave. How angry he'd been. "I mean, on the one hand, it made sense. We were digging something up at the place where he thinks his sister is buried. But also, that guy has a rage problem. He's dangerous."

"What are you saying?" Her voice was small, and Jason

wasn't sure whether the current he heard running beneath it was fear or anger.

"Jenna, Luke did this." He pointed to his eye. "He seemed capable of doing a lot worse. Rakesh was there. He saw it, too. Don't you think it's at least possible that he had something to do with Lacey's disappearance?"

"This is *Troy's* fault," Jenna answered stubbornly. Before Jason could protest, she switched her tack. "Let's look at the photo on my computer. Will you send it to me?"

"Here, it'll be easier if I just sign in." He flinched as he rose to switch places with her, the shifted weight resting on his sore muscles.

"Ugh, does it hurt a lot?" Her eyes were full of sympathy.

"Ah, it's not so bad."

She didn't buy his tough guy act. "Here, sit down, and I think there's a bag of peas or something in the freezer you can put on your eye. Let me run and grab it."

"You really don't have to."

"Jason, trust me, it'll help." He looked down at her hand, which was resting on his arm, and then back up. Their eyes met, and they both smiled shyly at the same time before she looked away. "I'll be right back."

He settled into the desk chair and waited for her computer to boot up, surveying the papers and knickknacks she had lying around as he did so. Some of her school notebooks were out, her handwriting small and neat and girlish. Her detailed outline for a European history class confirmed Jason's suspicion that she was an excellent student. Behind them was a frame, showing her and Lacey, arms around each other's shoulders, cheeks pressed together, twin huge grins illuminating their faces. It must have been taken during their sophomore year, before everything got so complicated. What would it have been like to know them then? Would Lacey have been so friendly, sharing her dreams of playing with a real band to his face, accompanying him to concerts, cracking him up as they watched YouTube videos together? Would Jenna have looked at him with those big trusting eyes, opened up to him about her friendship with Lacey? Or would he have been invisible to these beautiful popular girls, another nobody guy with a beat-up car and a weirdo record collection? Judging from this photo, with a party roaring behind them, the second option seemed more likely. He wondered what had changed, what had allowed both of them to connect with him. Was it something about them or was it something about him?

Opening the browser, he typed in *f-a-c* and Facebook popped up automatically. The mouse was hovering over the LOG OUT button when he noticed his profile picture. And then he had the sensation of being on one of those amusement-park rides where you drop fifteen stories in an instant. His stomach was falling at high speed, leaving his racing heart behind, hovering somewhere high in the air. Jason was logged in to Lacey's profile. Or rather *Jenna* was logged into Lacey's profile. He stared at the screen. There he was, his thumbnail-size face lonely as Lacey's only friend, the status updates that had been written specifically for him scrolling down the page. Had Lacey been here and used Jenna's computer?

He clicked the messages tab, and suddenly he was looking at the full-size photo of Lacey holding the necklace. Below that the heartfelt note he'd sent after following her instructions to go back to the cemetery. Jason couldn't breathe. *Me and J*

Money have been friends practically since we were born — we're family at this point. He'd wondered why Lacey had come to him and not to Jenna, but Jenna had been in on it from the beginning. Except . . . the idea was too much to handle, but what if Jenna had been *behind* it from the beginning? His head was swimming in confusion, but the second he laid eyes on the sheet of loose leaf buried under a stack of textbooks, he felt such an intense jolt of certainty his breath caught. Pushing the books aside, he saw his own handwriting.

> It was all turning gray
> It was all turning black
> Then you were there
> And you keep coming back
>
> These things tend to get ugly
> Or so I am told
> But now that you're here
> Everything's coming up gold
>
> Drive out, see the stars, in the car, we're falling hard
> Wake up, feel the sun, touch your hair, see your heart

It dawned on him then. Jenna had been the person in his room. Jenna *was* Lacey. At least she was the Lacey he knew. And he didn't want to think about the other Lacey or what had happened to her.

What kind of a sick person would do this? *You must think I'm crazy.* It was what Jenna had said the morning they'd first met. She kept repeating it at the coffee shop. He'd just assumed she meant crazy in a garden variety "Oh, sometimes I suffer from verbal diarrhea" way. Not crazy, like "I've been manipulating a stranger and impersonating my best friend and I probably belong in a mental ward" crazy.

The door began to creak open, and Jason sprang up, knocking the chair over. He'd forgotten about his broken body, but the movement as he spun around reminded him. Jenna was standing in the doorway holding a bag of frozen vegetables.

"What's wrong?" she asked innocently, and then her eyes went behind him to the computer screen, where Lacey's profile was still open. Then they saw the paper in his hand. Her face clouded over, and the vegetables fell to the ground with a thud. "It's not what you think," she said quickly, stepping toward him and shutting the door.

"Oh, really?" he kept his voice as quiet as he could. He still had no idea whether her parents were home. "What do I think? You could start by explaining that to me."

"Jason . . ."

"Have you been pretending to be Lacey this entire time? What kind of psycho would do that?"

"Please, just listen to me." She was on the edge of tears, but Jason didn't care.

"You're not even denying it!"

"You don't understand, it was the only way . . ."

"Is Lacey even *alive*?" He was shouting now. He couldn't stop himself. When she didn't answer, he pushed past her and charged down the stairs. "I have to get out of here." He could hear her footsteps behind him, but he was bigger and faster, and he was in the car before the revelation had even fully sunk in.

She followed him out the front door, calling for him, but all he could hear over the blood rushing in his ears was the roar of the engine as he peeled away from the curb. A block later, his phone started ringing. He pressed IGNORE but she kept calling, and it was only when he looked in his rearview mirror that he realized the persistent honking he heard was coming from her car behind him. She was chasing him. When he sped up, she did, too, waving wildly for him to stop. He hit a red light, and watched her frantically dialing him. She unbuckled her seat belt and started to get out of the car. Why wasn't the light changing? He looked left, looked right, and then floored it across the intersection, narrowly avoiding getting hit by an approaching truck, its horn drowning out the sound of his tires squealing. When the truck passed, he could see Jenna jump back in her car. Another car passed before the light turned green, obstructing the view between them, and Jason took the opportunity to hang a quick right into a crowded supermarket parking lot. He popped out of the driver's seat just in time to see the Toyota sail by, Jenna unaware of his diversion.

He was shaking when he got back in the car, and he drove home on side streets, still half expecting Jenna to appear behind him at any time. His phone kept ringing until he turned it off. At least he wasn't thinking about his throbbing eye or battered chest. He was thinking about Lacey and the deafening silence he'd been met with when he asked Jenna if she was still alive. How had he been so blind?

CHAPTER 24

On a deserted stretch of road, he pulled over. The nausea had been building since he'd seen the profile on Jenna's computer. Steadying himself against the side door, he retched, watching the cereal he'd eaten for breakfast come up. He took deep breaths when he finished, the fresh air and his empty stomach helping to clear his head.

It was sharpening into focus now. The cruel, horrible truth that Lacey was gone crystallized in his brain. More than ever, he felt like Hamlet. Hamlet thought he had it bad, he thought things couldn't get any worse, and then he learned that Ophelia was dead. Lacey was his Ophelia, and she was dead. For real this time. It had been Jenna all along. Every personal story he'd told, every intimate detail he'd shared, he'd been talking to Jenna, who had lied to him over and over again, online and to his face. He felt like he'd been betrayed by not one but two different people he cared about. The song lyrics he'd labored over lay crumpled on the floor of his car. Why had Jenna stolen them? Why had she done any of the things she did?

An answer was forming in his mind, but it was too ugly — too impossible. Something Jenna had said was bouncing around his skull like a pinball. *It's just . . . I've been on Roxy Choi's balcony, and you have to be pretty clumsy to fall off it backward.* He gagged again, but only bile was left in his throat. Maybe the real Lacey *had* been in danger. And maybe the danger came from her best friend. But it still didn't make sense. If Jenna had been responsible for Lacey's death, she'd want to conceal her involvement, not use a fake identity to invite a stranger to come sniffing around. Plus, Jenna might be off her rocker, but she wasn't violent. Jason was certain of that. But Jason's track record for certainty hadn't been very good lately.

The whirlwind events of the last week kept swirling around and tangling themselves up in knots. First there was Troy, who had hidden his rocky romantic relationship with Lacey from even his closest friend. Troy prostrate and weeping at Lacey's grave, apologizing over and over again. But the secrets Troy had been keeping weren't secret at all — Jason had found the video of Troy with Lacey in Luke's possession, which meant Luke knew they'd been together. Had he found out before or after Roxy Choi's party? Judging from his reaction to Max in the video, he'd known about Lacey's dalliances for a lot longer than anyone gave him credit for. And based on the fury Jason had been on the receiving end of at Lacey's grave, Luke was capable of some extreme violence. Jenna had defended him, blaming his rage on his sister's death, but Jenna was the least reliable of them all.

Despite that fact, Jason kept replaying the scene at her house, and her pleas to listen were tugging at him. He was struck with an inexplicable desire to turn his phone back on and call her. He wanted the truth — it was the only thing he wanted anymore — and she could give it to him. But she wouldn't. She was a liar. Jenna and Troy and Luke, all of them knowing more than they were letting on, all of them hiding their secrets behind their love of Lacey.

Lacey, who Jason had loved, too — or at least thought he could love — turned out to be the biggest lie of them all. And he had fallen for it. He felt disgusted with himself. How could he have been so stupid? He straightened out the song he'd been writing for Lacey and read it to himself silently one last time. The lyrics, once full of all the hope and happiness Jason possessed in the world, were hollow now. He ripped the paper again and again until it resembled nothing so much as confetti. Then he threw the tiny pieces by the side of the road and watched the wind whip them away.

He drove back to Oakdale like a zombie, and by the time he arrived at his house, he was so numb that he barely even noticed the station wagon parked outside. Until he saw Troy Palmer, clad in his garish Brighton High varsity jacket, leaning against the hood, that is. Then his attention perked right up. Troy didn't *look* like a murderer, but Jason knew that's what everyone said about serial killers.

Jason looked around the car for a weapon just in case. Rakesh had left food wrappers strewn about the passenger seat, and there were binders full of CDs everywhere. He'd never needed to defend himself against a six-foot-tall lacrosse-playing monster before yesterday, and not twenty-four hours later he was going to have to do it again. Lacking better options, he grabbed the plastic snow scraper he saw on the floor of the backseat. It hadn't done much in January when his windshield was coated in ice, but who knew, maybe it was waiting to fulfill its true destiny as an instrument of pain. When he stepped out of the car, Troy was approaching.

"What are you doing here?" Jason called out, looking around the street for neighbors. No one else was around.

"We need to talk about the necklace." Jason's shoulders stiffened. Troy was almost upon him now.

"How do you know about that?" Jason demanded. He gripped the snow scraper tightly in his right hand and tried to look as sure of himself as possible.

"It's Jason, right?" Troy stopped a few feet short of Jason, and put his hands up. "I'm not here to fight you, dude." Troy gestured to the scraper and smiled; his face was kinder than Jason expected. "Besides, if I were, that thing wouldn't do you much good. C'mon, let's go inside."

It was a command more than anything else, but Jason flexed his knuckles around the scraper's handle. "I'm not going anywhere with you until you tell me how you know my name and where I live."

"Should I call you Keith McKeller, guitar teacher to the stars?"

At the mocking reference to the pseudonym he'd used with Mr. Gray, Jason froze. Had he forgotten to block his number? How could he have been so careless?

As if reading his mind, Troy added, "You know *everyone* has caller ID, right? After you called Luke's house, it wasn't hard to track you down. We found you at the bridge that night."

So it had been Luke and Troy in the woods, Luke and Troy speeding off into the night. Were they working with Jenna? It didn't make sense, but *nothing* made sense anymore.

"I'm sorry about texting you like that," Troy said. Once again, Jason was surprised at the genuine note of apology in his voice. "It was Luke's idea."

Jason's brain was reeling. As he stood there speechless, Troy placed a hand on his shoulder. "So that's how I know who you are and where you live. Now it's my turn to ask a couple questions. How about you put this thing down, and we go inside."

More obediently than he would have liked, Jason lowered his arm and led Troy to a chair at his kitchen table. Perching on a stool at the counter, Jason's eyes darted around for blunt objects that could do more damage than the plastic snow scraper in a pinch.

"So . . ." Jason said awkwardly. By now, he was about 85 percent sure Troy hadn't come to harm him, but it wasn't much comfort. It was the type of thing you wanted 100 percent certainty on. While his visit to Jenna's house had thrown everything he knew about Lacey into doubt, it still seemed entirely plausible that Troy had been as dangerous to Lacey before she died as "Lacey" had led him to believe. The thought of the text messages wasn't helping.

"How did you know about me and Lacey?" Troy blurted out. "Who told you?"

"No one told me," Jason said. It was the truth.

"Then how did you know about the necklace? Luke told me you were digging up something at her grave. And I see he wasn't lying about kicking your butt." He nodded toward Jason's bruise.

"Why did you bury it?"

"I don't want to answer that until I know who you are. How were you connected to Lacey?"

Troy was watching him carefully. Jason mentally calculated the distance to the drawer where his mom kept the knives. He was closer, but Troy was in better shape. He thought he could make it there first, but he didn't want to test the theory. He'd stick to the truth in the hopes that it would help him avoid unnecessarily enraging the beast. "I wasn't," he said. "I mean, I thought I was. But I was wrong."

"Okay, but you must have known her. How?"

It was still sinking in that he really hadn't known her. Not even a little bit. It was Jenna the whole time. Jenna was the one he'd IM'd with so easily, the one who'd sent him the sweet and funny messages, the one convincing him he was the only one who could help "Lacey." Jason had been so foolish for ever having believed otherwise. Troy looked at him expectantly, waiting for an answer.

"It's complicated."

Troy rolled his eyes. "You're going to have to do better than that."

Maybe Jason should tell him everything. After all, it would be a relief to get all of the secrets and the lies off his chest. If he couldn't just walk away from the situation, at least he could unload. His whole relationship with Lacey had been a sham; he no longer owed her any sort of discretion. But the idea of spilling his guts to a complete stranger didn't exactly appeal, especially since, Jason reminded himself, that stranger might be a violent psychopath.

"I talked to Lacey online."

"On Facebook?"

"Yeah."

"When did it start?"

There was an urgency to the question, and at first Jason was shocked that Troy understood the strange nature of his relationship with Lacey, but then he realized the question rose from his insecurities about whether or not Lacey had been faithful to him. "It wasn't while you were with her," Jason said with a hollow laugh.

"Did she tell you that we were together?"

"Not exactly. Why did you insist on keeping it a secret?" It was one of many questions Jason couldn't figure out, but it bothered him more than the others. If he'd been dating Lacey, he would have screamed it from the rooftops. Though, he supposed, he sort of had been dating Lacey, or believed he had, and he'd kept silent about it. At her request. Jenna's request. The thoughts were swirling in his head, making it difficult for him to focus on what Troy was saying; he was going to have to shut off his inner monologue unless he wanted to lose his mind.

"Um, do I need to remind you what Luke is like when he's mad? Besides, it wasn't just me. Lacey didn't want to tell him, either. She was afraid he'd kill me. We came up with, like, all these codes and stuff." He smiled slightly, as if recollecting a memory. "We called the tree house in my backyard the Kissing Club. KC for short." It explained the random letters on the necklace, the Casey phone call Max had witnessed. But there were still more important questions to answer. "Don't you think it's kind of weird? What difference did it make to him who she dated?" His pitch kept going up at the end of his questions, making him sound like a whiny child. To make matters worse, Troy had an authoritative deep bass. That night in Jenna's room, when they'd originally agreed to begin following Troy, Jason had pictured their sleuthing ending in an interrogation in which he masterfully outsmarted Troy, forcing him to own up to everything he had done. This was a far cry from the scene he had imagined.

Troy looked at him like he was crazy. "You really must not have known Lacey."

"What's that supposed to mean?"

"For someone so smart, she could be all kinds of stupid. She'd trust anyone and everyone. There was no one else looking out for her — people see a pretty girl with a big heart, and they think they can get anything they want from her. Luke protected her from them. Sometimes I think . . ."

Troy began to choke up. Jason had watched him cry the other night, heaving sobs at the base of the memorial, and he sensed if he kept Troy talking, he was going to get an encore performance. Still, Jason pressed him. "Sometimes you think what?"

"If he did find out about me and Lacey, if he put a stop to it, maybe things would have been different."

Jason's heart was pounding. Troy was about to confess to the murder. Maybe this had been Jenna's plan all along. "Different how?" He asked the question as steadily as he could, but his eyes once again went to the knife drawer. On the verge of tears, he had the effect of a gentle giant, but if he'd killed Lacey, whom he'd apparently loved, there was no telling what he might do to Jason after revealing his darkest secret.

"Maybe she'd still be here." Now he was full-on crying, the tears streaming down his cheeks. "Maybe she wouldn't have killed herself."

CHAPTER 25

Wait, what?" Jason felt like a starlet at an awards ceremony hearing someone else's name called for best actress when she was certain she'd win; despite his best efforts, his face betrayed all of the confusion and disappointment that struck him with Troy's revelation. But Troy didn't notice.

"She killed herself because of me. If I hadn't let the secrets build up like that, she'd still be alive." Instinctively, Jason grabbed the box of tissues his mom kept on the windowsill and brought them to the table. Troy took one gratefully. His breath was shallow and the tears were streaming down his cheeks; Jason was seized by a desire to snap a photo of the oversize jock turned blubbery child. He'd be a hero to emo kids everywhere who were tormented by guys like Troy on a daily basis. Jason couldn't remember the last time he'd wept openly, but he'd watched Troy do it twice this week.

"Do you, um, want a glass of water?"

Troy looked up at him, his blue eyes clear through the pooling tears. "That'd be great," he sniffled. Jason brought it to the table, and Troy gulped it down, and slowly the crying subsided.

Jason sat across from him now. "I'm sorry, I know this stuff is hard for you to talk about, but can you explain what you mean? I thought Lacey's fall was supposed to have been an accident."

"I guess she just got sick of all the secrets," Troy said slowly. "At Roxy's party, she was a total mess. We got a few minutes alone, and she said, 'We have to tell Luke about what's going on between us *tonight*,' but what she didn't know was that Luke was on the warpath. Mr. Jericho, our craptastic math teacher, was trying to get it so Luke couldn't start unless he brought up his grade to a B, which was not happening. Usually coach can get us out of stuff like that, but Mr. Jerkwad wasn't having it, so coach told Luke he had to start getting tutored in trig. By Roxy's party, he was ready to kill someone."

Troy was speaking figuratively, but Jason wondered how ready.

"So I started to tell her, but she wouldn't listen. She was like, 'It has to be now, I can't live like this anymore,' and I . . ." Troy paused, looking stricken, "I told her to stop being such a drama queen." His face crumbled. "It was the last thing I ever said to her." Jason waited as Troy put himself together. Could Lacey have really killed herself? Jenna was so certain she hadn't, but Jenna no longer qualified as a reliable source. As if Troy could read his thoughts, he continued, "Her friend Jenna found us. That was the other reason Lacey didn't want everyone to know about us. She was worried about what Jenna would do."

The queasiness Jason had felt in his car earlier returned. "Why?"

"I don't want to sound conceited, but Jenna kind of had a thing for me. I had no idea, because she never said a word when she was around me, but Lacey told me. It started when they were like eleven or something — they'd spy on me and Luke when we were at the Grays' and they called me penguin because

I wore a tux to someone's bar mitzvah when I was in seventh grade. I literally don't even remember it."

Ask her if she still has the penguin's shirt in the back of her closet. His skin was crawling now.

"Lacey really cared about Jenna, and she didn't want her to get hurt. She made me go out of my way to be super friendly to her whenever I was around, which was fine; Jenna's a nice girl."

"Depends what you mean by nice." It was only after the words were out of his mouth that Jason realized he had spoken them aloud.

"You know Jenna?" Troy sounded surprised.

"I'm sorry — I didn't mean to interrupt your story. What happened after Jenna found you guys?"

All the hesitance Troy had exhibited when he first sat down was gone now. He was caught up in the relief of confession. He hadn't talked to anyone about this, and Jason could tell he wasn't the type of guy who was meant to keep his feelings bottled up, even if that's what everyone expected of him.

"Jenna said she needed to talk to her. At first, Lacey was like, 'We can talk here, there's something I need to tell you anyway,' but I was shaking my head, trying to get her to shut up. So then she pulled Lacey aside, and I had to pretend like we were in the middle of a normal conversation. I kept waiting for another chance to get Lacey alone because we weren't done figuring out what to do about Luke, but she disappeared. And then, the next morning, when I realized what happened . . ." He'd gone hoarse, but he didn't cry this time. He went on flatly, "I knew it was my fault."

"Troy, did you see Jenna again that night?" Once the question was past his lips, Jason realized he was terrified of the answer. He didn't believe Jenna was capable of murder because he didn't *want* her to be. In spite of everything, he was surprised to find that he still liked Jenna.

He shook his head. "I don't remember."

"It's important."

"Dude, I don't get it. You just told me you barely knew Lacey. Why do you care so much? About any of this? Why did you call her house?"

"I don't think Lacey killed herself." It was the simplest reply.

Suddenly, the big man on campus bravado was back. "And how would you know?"

"Because I think someone pushed her."

CHAPTER 26

*T*roy stared at Jason with a mixture of confusion and hurt, but before he could speak, something barreled across the kitchen and tackled him.

"How you like that?" Rakesh yelped as he ground Troy's shoulder into the kitchen floor.

"Rakesh! He didn't do anything!" But it was too late. Troy had knocked Rakesh off of him and pinned him down.

"Who are you?" Troy growled. Jason pulled him off and both boys scrambled to their feet.

"Both of you, calm down!" The effort of separating them had inflamed the pain in Jason's ribs. He stood, panting, and then turned to Rakesh. "Jesus, what are you doing here?"

"That's the thanks I get for rescuing you from this psychopath?"

"Seriously, who is this guy?"

"Troy, Rakesh, Rakesh, Troy. There, now everyone knows each other. Rock, what's the deal?"

"I could ask you the same question. You haven't answered any of my texts in the last two hours. So I came by to make sure everything was okay, because last I checked, the Brighton lacrosse team was out for your blood. And then lo and behold, Mr. Brighton Lacrosse himself is sitting at your kitchen table. What was I supposed to do?"

"Not break into my house?"

"I didn't break in — I have keys!"

"Why didn't you knock?"

"There's a car outside with a bumper sticker that has a skull and crossbones made out of lacrosse sticks that says 'Brighton' underneath. I called you twice from outside — why does your phone keep going to voice mail?"

"I turned it off."

"Why? What's going on here?"

"That's what I want to know," Troy grumbled.

"Rock, Lacey's dead," and then when he saw Rakesh start toward Troy again, he quickly added, "Troy didn't do it! Troy, I promised I'd explain everything, but I'm going to have to start at the beginning. Can we all be civil to each other?" Rakesh and Troy eyed each other warily, but they both assented. "All right, good. This is gonna take a while, so let's at least sit down."

And so Jason began with his message to Lacey and the response he got three months later. Their easy rapport, the way he fell for her. How he found the obituary. The run-in with Jenna at the memorial, and Lacey's pleading e-mails to him implicating Troy. Troy listened to all of it quietly, interrupting here and there with a question. As Jason went on, knowing what he now knew, the story sounded stranger and stranger. Why hadn't he realized what was happening sooner? He carefully avoided eye contact as he described tailing Troy to the cemetery, and Rakesh eagerly took over the narration when he got to Luke Gray's attack the following morning.

And then there was nothing left except the thing he hadn't

had the nerve to say out loud yet. "And now I know Lacey was never the one Facebooking me. It was Jenna all along."

Rakesh gasped. "Hold up. *What?*"

"Yeah. I went over there this morning, and I used her computer. She was signed into Lacey's profile. Jenna's been lying to me — to everyone — this whole time. She's the one who sent the messages, the one who told me to break into Luke's car. She's been setting Troy up."

He let the news sink in. "So you're saying *Jenna* killed Lacey?" Jason was so grateful for the skepticism in Rakesh's voice he could have hugged him. It was like Lacey all over again. There had to be some other explanation.

"Sorry, can we go back a second?" Troy's face was twisted up, like he was remembering something. "Can I see the messages you got from 'Lacey'?"

The air quotations he made with his fingers caused Jason to wince, but all the same he went to his room to retrieve his laptop. When he got back downstairs, Rakesh was standing in the hallway whispering into his phone. "No, tell them not to come. . . . Because . . ." He turned and saw Jason. "I'll call you back. *Don't* come here."

"What was that?"

"Um, nothing."

Jason set down his computer in the living room and logged in to Facebook. "Rakesh, why are you being shady?"

"I'm not being shady."

"Rock."

"Fine, I kind of sort of may have invited some people over. But it was before I knew what was going on. Don't worry, I've rescinded all of the invitations."

"What's *wrong* with you? I told you I wasn't having a party tonight."

"It seemed kind of like you wanted me to invite people anyway."

"It didn't seem like that at all!"

"We can just chalk it up to a failure to communicate."

"I could seriously kill you."

"Look, you have to admit, this is sort of your fault."

"*My* fault? Are you kidding?"

"If you'd just answered your text messages, we could have avoided the confusion."

Before Jason could sputter a reply, Troy cut in. "I hate to interrupt you two crazy kids, but can we get back to business?" He gestured to the computer. Still fuming, Jason logged in to Facebook and opened his messages. And then he blinked. And blinked again. This couldn't be happening.

Rakesh peered over his shoulder. "Wait." He drew out the word as the reality of what Jason had already recognized dawned on him. "Oh my god, all the Lacey messages are gone."

Frantically, Jason typed her name into the search bar. The memorial page came up, but her profile was nowhere to be found. He put his forehead to the coffee table. "Jenna," he breathed. "She must have deleted them and then deleted the profile."

"Oh, there's something I forgot to mention," Rakesh said nervously. Jason lifted his head to glower at him, but didn't say a word. "It's *possible* that I invited her to your party tonight."

"This is a joke. You're playing a joke on me. That's what's happening, right? You're messing with me?" He'd started to laugh, but it sounded raw, almost animal, the type of thing you heard from crazy people on public buses, and Rakesh was slowly backing away.

"It was before I knew she had a Single White Female thing going and might have murdered her best friend. If it helps, I really thought you guys might have something together."

"It doesn't help. Why would that help?"

Troy was not amused, either. "Can you guys focus? Please? When I'm the person telling you not to act like children, you have a problem."

"But . . ." Rakesh started.

Jason cut him off with dagger eyes. "Troy's right. We need a plan. Starting with you need to keep Jenna from coming here. How did you even invite her in the first place?"

"I friended her."

"Of course you did." Jason was practically shaking with rage.

Rakesh took out his phone. "I didn't give her your address. But . . ." He looked up nervously. Jason waited. "She said she already had it."

"Don't answer!" Jason remembered the way she'd looked in his rearview mirror when she was chasing him. Desperate. Her showing up at his house was the last thing he needed.

"I wasn't going to. As if I need your help blowing someone off. Jesus, these messages. She really wants you to call her. You're not gonna be able to avoid her forever."

Before they could descend further into an argument, Troy interrupted. "He only needs to avoid her until we figure out what to do. Jason, do you have any record of the messages she sent you as Lacey?"

Jason tried to remember, but came up short. He shook his head. "I thought we were all on the same side."

"Well, except for you," Rakesh added pointedly to Troy. "And Luke. Who's the worst."

"Dude, are you really gonna talk to me like that after what just happened in the kitchen?"

"Troy, I know he's your friend, but Rock has a point about Luke. I think he's involved in this somehow."

"Oh, that's just perfect coming from you. First of all, your batting average when it comes to getting suspicious is a little spotty. Exhibit A." Troy pointed to himself. "And second of all, it's obvious you just don't want to consider the possibility that your girlfriend may have done this." It was like he hadn't sat in front of Jason weeping just an hour ago; when it came to his teammates, Troy was pure alpha male.

Jason stood and turned toward him. "For the last freaking time, Jenna is *not* my girlfriend. But while we're on the subject of willful blindness, let's talk about Luke. You said yourself he'd have gone ballistic if he knew about you and Lacey, but he *did* know about you and Lacey. I found the video in his car. We know he's violent because, um, hello? My face. And I'm sorry, but I'm just not buying that the way he looked out for his sister was normal. I saw the way he nearly ripped Max's head off for just talking to her this summer, and it was way beyond bros being bros."

His fight with Jenna this morning, his injuries, the way his world kept turning upside down like a snow globe — these things should have left him spent. Instead, they were having the opposite effect, transforming Jason into a commanding presence who had no problem standing up to a guy practically twice his size. Troy clearly wasn't used to it, either — he was stunned into silence. Just before Jason lost his momentum, his eyes widened. "The video." He sprinted back up the stairs, returning breathless. "I got it from Luke's car. They can't destroy the hard copy." Troy and Rakesh gathered behind him, and he plugged the drive into his computer.

He waited until Troy had seen the whole thing before opening his mouth. Instead of drawing attention to Luke's unbridled aggression, which he sensed was a losing game, he brought up the cameraman. "The guy who shot this, Sully. What's his real name again?"

"John Sullivan."

"Yeah, him. Is he a friend of yours?"

"He's on the team, so yeah."

Behind Troy's back, Rakesh rolled his eyes.

"So then he must be a friend of Luke's, too."

"What's your point?"

"How'd Luke get this?"

"I don't know. Maybe sweet innocent Jenna stole it from him and planted it on him."

Jason resisted the urge to defend her. There was no point. "What would Sully have done after he shot this? No offense, but I feel like a guy who secretly records his 'friend' fighting with their girlfriend isn't all that likely to keep someone else's secrets out of the goodness of his heart. Who does he like better, you or Luke?"

"Luke," Troy admitted reluctantly. Before he could say more, the doorbell rang.

"Oh goodie," Jason said sarcastically to Rakesh, "the party's starting."

When Jason opened the door, Gabe Wyffels was standing there, his goofy grin plastered across his face. "Hey, man," Gabe said, peeking into the hallway behind Jason. "Am I early?"

Jason realized he had no idea what time it was or where the day had gone. Darkness had settled around his house, and the temperature had dropped. The cool air felt good on his bare arms, and for a moment he imagined slipping outside into the night, blasting Titus Andronicus from the Subaru, and driving somewhere far, far away. Rakesh sidled up behind him. "Gabe, buddy, good to see you. Listen . . ." He slung his arm around Gabe's shoulders and began guiding him back to his car. Jason tuned out the murmured excuses and padded into his yard for some fresh air.

He took his phone out of his pocket and turned it back on to check the time. How had he gotten himself into this mess? Lacey was supposed to make his quiet little world better, not flip it on its head and toss a grenade into the middle of it. The first girl he'd ever truly cared about turned out to be a hoax propagated by his first female friend. His best friend was unplanning the party of the century — to which he hadn't even really been invited — while a rival school's golden boy waited in his living room for his directions. The old Jason, the one who was invisible to girls, happy to spend his Saturday afternoons seeking out new music, whose problems consisted of boredom, that guy had no idea how good he had it. Gabe Wyffels's taillights disappeared down the block, and Rakesh returned to Jason's side.

"I'm sorry about tonight," he said quietly. "Are you all right?"

The contrition in his tone stirred up all of Jason's exhausted hopelessness. His eyes stung, and a lump formed in his throat. It seemed foolish now that he knew his Lacey was a hoax, but grief for losing her was coursing through him. Before the emotion could bubble over, Troy-style, the phone in his hand came to life. There were a dozen new text messages and half as many voice mails. Facebook, texting, looking up something online in an instant. These things had always been so comforting to him, but for the first time he understood why his mom found technology so frustrating. You couldn't pause for a minute to take a breath, or slow anything down. Even when you tried to shut the world out, you couldn't escape the fact that it was carrying on around you. Something Jenna said the first time they met popped into his head. *Lacey's gone, and Facebook keeps happening.* Thinking about it now, he shuddered.

He scrolled through the texts Rakesh had sent.

2:45 Imma invite some people to your house. I'll keep it small.
3:22 Maybe not that small.
3:24 15-150 people
3:29 8 pm good?
3:57 Pinata good idea or best idea?
4:17 Taking your silence as a yes.
4:38 Ok, now I'm worried. Are you ok?

Rakesh grinned sheepishly, and even Jason cracked a smile at the piñata line.

There was one from his mother, reminding him to water her plants, and signed, like all of her texts, "Love, Mom." And then there were four from Jenna.

2:37 J, I can explain, please just pick up the phone

2:50 PLEASE call me I need to talk to you

3:05 I'm so sorry, we needed your help. There was no other way.

4:58 K now I am stalking you, but DON'T DELETE my vm. Listen & call me back.

All but one of the voice messages were from Jenna. Jason sighed.

"Are you going to call her back?"

"I don't know. I guess I have to listen to the messages first. But not until I get some food." Hunger gnawed away at him. He'd eaten a banana in the kitchen with Troy, but before that he'd left the contents of his stomach by the side of the road. The Tylenol he'd taken that morning had worn off hours ago. He felt a little like a walking corpse, but he knew he wouldn't be able to rest until he understood why Jenna had done this to him. So maybe Lacey was nothing more than a fantasy. That didn't mean he couldn't help her. It was what any nice guy would do.

CHAPTER 27

There was an argument when it emerged that Troy wanted to go see Sully alone. "You didn't even know Lacey," he said, "and Sully will freak if a stranger shows up asking questions about one of his videos. Let me handle this."

Jason told Troy he wouldn't even know about the video if it weren't for him, and besides, he had a right to know why Jenna was manipulating him. Troy scoffed at this line of reasoning, and then Jason bluffed. "You think Sully's the only one with a camera phone? Jenna said following you was worthless unless we got proof." He removed his phone from his pocket and held it under Troy's nose. "Unless you want the entire Internet to see you crying like a child, Rakesh and I are coming along."

Troy begrudgingly agreed after that, and Jason made a note to try blackmail again sometime.

And then they were in Troy's car, barreling toward Brighton at fifteen miles above the speed limit. They picked up a pizza on the way, the hot cheese burning the roof of Jason's mouth as he tore into it. Food kept the dizziness at bay, and filling his stomach provided a second wind.

"Who's *we*?" he shouted over the B.o.B blasting from Troy's speakers.

"What?" Troy answered.

"*We*. Jenna said '*we* needed your help' in her text message. Who is she talking about?"

"I thought we agreed homegirl is crazy," Rakesh said from the backseat. "She probably means Lacey. Or maybe she's referring to an imaginary friend."

Jason chewed, hesitant to voice his theory lest Troy throw him out of the car. But it was coming together in his mind. Luke and Jenna made the perfect team. They knew everything there was to know about Lacey. They had access to her history, her photographs, even what she was wearing when her body was found. Luke had known about Lacey and Troy, so he'd murdered Lacey and framed her boyfriend to get revenge. Jenna was jealous that her best friend was secretly dating the guy she'd been after since they were in middle school.

But Jason kept running up against the fact that Jenna didn't seem capable of violence. That wasn't misguided affection for her talking; he sensed deep in his gut there was something they were all missing. Jason was convinced that piece would explain his involvement, because so far nothing else had even come close to helping him understand what Jenna and Luke wanted with him.

Jenna's messages kept creeping back into his head. *I'm so sorry, we needed your help. There was no other way.* No other way to what? His impulse to call her and hear her out may have been crazy, but it wasn't going away.

"What did Sully say?" Jason asked, reaching into the backseat for another slice. "When you asked him about the video."

"I told him I knew about the footage from the summer and I wanted to see it all. He texted me back and said I should come over."

"Did he say 'come over,' like, 'we're friends, and I'll show you anything you want to see,' or was it, 'come over,' like, 'come the video?'"

"It was 'come over' like it was a text message. Look, when we get there, you have to relax with this Sherlock Holmes business. And unless you want to get beat up again, you better not say anything to him about Luke — Sully's small, but he's vicious."

The food and darkness lulled Jason into a disoriented daze, and he couldn't have said whether it was minutes or hours that passed before they arrived in Brighton. Climbing out of the car, he couldn't believe it had only been this morning that he'd sprinted out of Jenna's room; only two nights ago that he'd bonded with Jenna as they watched Troy. Like so many other things in Jason's life, time had twisted into an unfamiliar force with questionable intentions.

Sully's house was larger than Jenna's, almost palatial. The three boys marched past a black BMW parked in the driveway and then the silver Lexus hidden behind it. John Sullivan. It was the sort of name that should have a number after it, and Jason guessed he probably did. When they reached a door in the back, Troy opened it without knocking and then turned to Jason and Rakesh and held a finger to his lips. They followed him up two dark staircases, Jason clutching the banister to guide him. When they reached the brightly lit third floor, a stocky guy in sweatpants and a Giants T-shirt looked up from the enormous TV he was sprawled in front of.

"Who are they?" he asked, nodding in Jason's direction. His voice was instantly recognizable from the video.

"Jason, Rakesh, this is Sully."

Sully lumbered to his feet and surveyed them. Jason tried to picture how he must look through someone else's eyes: His hair, he was sure, was sticking out in a million directions, and his bruised face couldn't be helping with his credibility. Next to him, Rakesh, slender, striking, held his shoulders back and stared Sully down defiantly. Sully didn't flinch.

"What can I do for you, Troy?" he drawled, eyes lingering on Rock.

"Where's the video?"

"Now, what video could you be talking about?"

"Sully, I swear, don't mess with me. I saw the video you made from that night at Luke's. I want to know what you did with it."

"Oh, you mean the video where you humiliate Luke's sister in front of all of his friends? That one?"

"I never humilia . . ." Sully's face lit up with glee at the response, and Troy composed himself, shoving his hands into his pockets. It reminded Jason of the person he'd seen in Sully's home movie — all controlled fury, none of the weepiness Troy had displayed so unabashedly. It was like with Jenna: You think you see someone, and then the light shifts, and they have a whole new face. "What'd you do with it?"

"How about you explain something to me first? Did you really think no one was gonna find out? That using that Max kid was going to work as an excuse forever? Please. You think you and Lacey were being so stealthy, but *everyone* knew."

"What do you care?"

"That's my team, man! Gray was going to find out, and he was going to kill you, and it was going to kill our season."

Typical, Jason thought. *A girl is dead, I'm being stalked by a psycho, and he's talking about lacrosse. Glad we've all got our priorities straight.* But Troy was unfazed. "What'd you do with it?" he asked again.

"I should be asking you the same question."

"What's that supposed to mean?"

"I don't have the video, Troy. I haven't had it since I lost my phone. So do you want to tell me how you somehow managed to watch it? Let me guess, it has something to do with these clowns." He sneered at Rakesh, but it was Jason who answered him.

"When'd you lose your phone?"

Sully took a step toward him. "September."

"What happened?"

"I left it in my book bag during practice, and when we were done, it was gone. Probably Hugo."

"Who's Hugo?"

"The retarded janitor."

"Jesus, Sully." Troy rolled his eyes exasperatedly. "Hugo's not retarded. And he didn't steal your phone."

"Because you did?"

Jason interrupted again. "Who else had access to the locker room? Did anyone know what was on there?"

For the first time, Sully actually looked him in the eye. "Other than Hugo and the coaches, no one goes in the locker room while we're in practice. Except sometimes the coaches give their keys to the captains. Like Palmer here."

"Or like Luke Gray?" Jason had ignored Troy's warning not to ask questions, and now he was violating the second rule. "Could he have stolen your phone?"

"Relax, Jason," Troy said sharply as Sully's face darkened with anger. "You, too, Sully."

"Don't freaking tell me to relax. You bring this tool into my house, you let him talk about Luke like this. Seriously, who are you?"

Now he got in Jason's face, and Rakesh quickly stepped in. "Your boy Luke caught me by surprise yesterday, but if I'd seen him coming, he'd be a dead man right now. You will, too, if you step to my friend again."

Jason felt a surge of gratitude, followed by an urge to laugh. Rakesh was always talking about fighting guys, but until yesterday, Jason was pretty sure it had never actually happened. Strangely enough, Sully retreated, though he continued to glare at Jason.

"Dude, I'm not trying to fight you," Jason said. "And I mean no disrespect, but I found the video in Luke's glove compartment — and . . ."

"Oh, you're the one who broke into his car?" Sully started toward him again, but Troy restrained him.

The words kept spilling out of Jason's mouth. "If you care about Luke and your *team* at all, you'll tell me what you know, because otherwise I'll go to the police and tell them Luke killed his sister, and your season will be over." It was a wild bluff, but Jason's poker face was getting better. Sully looked nervously from Troy to Jason, briefly at Rakesh, and then back to Troy.

"Is that what happened?" He was starting to break, Jason could tell.

"What aren't you telling us, Sully?"

He sank into the couch and placed his hands on his knees.

"He didn't need the video, man. He already knew."

"What do you mean?"

Sully's eyes kept darting between his visitors, like a trapped animal looking for an escape route. "I tried to cover for you," he said to Troy. "I told him I heard something about his sister and that punk Max. I mean, I thought you were going to hit it and quit it like everyone else did." Troy charged toward him, and Sully leapt to his feet, ready to fight, but he was quickly overpowered. Troy's fist hovered in the air while he used his other hand to hold Sully down.

"Say another word about Lacey, and I'll make sure you never walk again, you smarmy little daddy's boy." His voice was quiet, but sharp enough to cut glass. "Now tell me when you talked to Luke about it."

Sully stared up at him defiantly. Troy knocked his head against the floor and growled, "*When?*"

Beaten, Sully muttered, "The day before Roxy Choi's party."

The buzzing from Jason's pocket was right on cue. Jenna. Again. He pressed IGNORE, but a minute later it started to ring again. Rakesh couldn't keep the smugness out of his voice when he asked Troy whether he still believed Luke was innocent. Troy shot him a withering glance and then released his grip on Sully and stood up.

"You think it was Luke?" he asked.

The phone in his hand flashed that Jenna had left another voice mail. Sully lumbered to his feet. "When did you replace your phone?" Jason asked quietly.

He scoffed. "The day after I lost it. I can't live without a phone."

Jenna's words came back to him. *John Sullivan . . . He's on the lacrosse team and he's always got his camera out. It's so annoying.*

"Did you film anything the night of Roxy's party?"

"I don't remember."

"What do you mean you don't remember?"

He laughed drily but no one joined him. "That night was kind of a blur."

Troy smacked him on the back of the head, and Sully's hand shot out in a jab, but Troy was out of the way.

Rakesh and Jason exchanged an uneasy glance. Rakesh voiced the question for both of them. "Yo, is drinking some sort of capital crime in Brighton?"

"During the season it is," Troy answered, still glaring at Sully.

"Well, can you check? Would you still have it?"

"I never delete anything." He moved to the gleaming monitor in the corner. "After my phone disappeared, I started backing everything up." Sully clicked through his hard drive, and asked Troy if he remembered what night the party had been.

"October fourth," he said quickly.

"What do we have here?" Sully said. He opened the video, and they assembled behind him, attention fixed on the screen.

At first it was a party, like any other party. A few kids told Sully to piss off, someone gave him the finger, and from the side of the frame, you could see him returning the gesture. "Hate that kid," he muttered. The air went out of the room the moment Lacey appeared on the screen. She'd looked so happy and alive in the other video, but here her expression was tired and drawn, distress visible in all of her movements. *What was she so upset about?* Jason wondered. She fingered her necklace distractedly as her eyes wandered around the room, and then Troy was at her side. He leaned over and said something into her ear, then she strode off as he followed closely behind her, looking around him to make sure he wasn't being watched, somehow missing Sully and his camera.

"This was right before she told me we had to tell Luke," Troy explained. "We went up to the balcony to talk."

Sully began to wander around the house. In the living room, he focused on a couple, apparently underclassmen, kissing on the sofa. Rakesh burst out laughing as the girl looked up, mortification all over her face. "Turn that off," she protested, but Sully just laughed and walked away.

"Classy," Jason said sarcastically.

Sully held up his hands defensively, "Hey, I wasn't the one going at it on someone else's couch."

And then suddenly Jenna was on camera, in a doorway, checking her phone. She looked up and saw Sully coming toward her. "Hey, have you seen Lacey?" she asked.

"Yeah, she went upstairs with *Troy*," he slurred.

"Why are you always trying to start something?" She reached out and batted the camera away. "Turn that thing off." For whatever reason, Sully complied.

"That must have been right before she came upstairs," Troy said.

"Yeah, but did you see how confused she was when Sully was trying to tell her you guys were together? I don't think she knew." Hope flickered inside of Jason. He wanted so much to be wrong about Jenna.

"Maybe Lacey told her when they were alone."

Jason tried to focus. There was something off about it. "Sully, is there more?"

"Yeah, I have two other videos from that night. Now I sort of remember taping that one, but the rest of that party is pretty hazy. I have no idea what happened."

"Let's find out."

CHAPTER 28

When the video started up again, the music had gotten louder, and the camera was less steady. A meaty guy in a Brighton lacrosse jacket was badly impersonating a math teacher, pushing imaginary glasses up his nose, pulling at a necktie that wasn't there, and spouting nonsense about equations. They could hear Sully laughing loudly, but the comedian was looking next to him at someone they couldn't see.

"I hate that guy," the invisible man said; Jason could tell he wasn't smiling as he spoke.

"That's Luke?"

"Yep," Troy said. "We were all trying to make him feel better about Jericho. Though I doubt Springer's method actually worked."

The camera turned toward Luke, who nodded at Sully and quietly asked him to turn it off. An instant later, the screen went black.

"One more," Troy said.

Jason's pulse began to race, and something in him twisted up. What if the third video was just Sully taping the activity in his coat pocket? Jenna and Luke. They killed Lacey, and then they stalked him, manipulated him, used him as a puppet. But the *why* lingered, a thorny knot he could barely get a hand around, much less untangle. Jenna had a crush on Troy and was angry at her friend for going behind her back. Luke was crazy overprotective and felt betrayed. But these were motives for writing an all-caps screed on someone's Facebook wall, not for murder. And they didn't explain what Jason was doing here, in John Sullivan IV's playroom, waiting to watch a grainy iPhone video of kids he'd barely met.

Jason still hadn't listened to Jenna's messages. Worse than seeing nothing on the tape, he suddenly realized, would be seeing proof that Jenna hurt Lacey. She was dishonest and probably sick, but he didn't want to believe she was a killer. He *couldn't* believe it. He wanted to tell them to pause; he wished he could put everything on hold, just for a second, just until his head was straight, but the movie was rolling.

"Can you fast-forward through this part?" Troy's impatience hummed through his entire body, you could see it in his tapping foot, his pursed lips. He had none of Jason's reluctance to find out what had happened, only a thirst for the truth.

Sully rolled his eyes, but did as he was told. This video was longer than the others, almost twenty minutes according to the scrollbar at the bottom of the screen. They were nearly halfway through when they got to a figure they recognized. "There, stop," Troy and Jason said in unison.

It was Lacey, standing in the dimly lit hallway. The picture was out of focus, most of the shot was blackness, but Lacey's chin being filmed from below was unmistakable. "Now I remember," Sully said, his brow furrowed with concentration. "I couldn't find my phone when we were leaving. I thought someone stole it again, and I was freaking out. Spencer found it in the hallway before we left."

"Shhh!" Jason silenced him. Lacey was talking. Troy leaned down and turned the volume as high as it would go.

"Go back," he commanded. Sully rewound until the phone dropped from his hand. They watched him scamper down the stairs and saw the feet of Arla Summers and whatever guy she was with pass through the frame. Then Lacey's blurry face filled the screen.

Jason held his breath. ". . . don't care who you tell," she was saying. "I'm tired of keeping these secrets. They'll get over it. They love me. Which is more than I can say for you. I thought you were my friend, but everyone else was right, you're disgusting."

"Watch what you say to me." The disembodied male voice was familiar, but Jason couldn't place it. From the look on Troy's face, he couldn't, either.

"I'm not afraid of you," Lacey said, but a second later, you could see fear register in her eyes. "Max, don't . . ."

"Luke," Rakesh said.

Jason saw spots. Maybe he had heard wrong. Troy confirmed he hadn't: "Are you deaf? She just said *Max*."

"No, Luke is *here*." He pointed, and sure enough, Luke stood in Sully's doorway, white as a sheet, the darkness of the hallway at his back. His eyes flitted uneasily between his friends and the two kids he'd attacked the day before.

Troy addressed him gently. "How long have you —"

"I'm going to kill you," Luke wailed, barreling toward them.

Before Jason could be sure which "you" he was referring to, Troy stepped in front of the group and locked arms with his cocaptain.

"You think you can lie to me? I know all about you!" Luke swung wildly, and Troy absorbed the blows to his shoulders and chest, only lifting his hand protectively when Luke's fists approached his face.

"Dude, calm down," Troy managed in between punches. "Let me explain."

"Don't bother explaining. I knew about you and Lacey. Why didn't you protect her? She needed you. And now you're here, with this guy. . . ." He gestured to Jason and then finally relented, dropping his hands to his sides, panting. Sully stood next to him and pulled him gently backward, out of arm's reach of Troy, who was rubbing his biceps where Luke had been hitting him.

"Let me explain," Troy repeated finally. "Jason just wants to help Lacey. That video. Did you see it?"

Jason came to his aid. "She didn't fall, Luke."

"I know," he said mournfully. Jason realized he thought she jumped. Because of Troy. That was why he'd been so aggressive at the grave site; he was protecting his friend. It was the only thing left he could do.

"She didn't do it to herself, either," Jason added. Luke looked up at him, and for the first time Jason saw something other than fury in his eyes. There was all the sadness, all the loss pooled up and trapped there. Now he understood Jenna had been right: Luke really was torn up over the death of his sister.

Luke looked uneasily at Troy. "What's he talking about?"

It took him a minute to answer. Like Jason, he was still wrapping his mind around it, parsing through what they'd just seen. "It was Max." He started to explain the video.

Jason's head was spinning. He went back to the beginning as well. So much had happened since he'd first begun talking to Lacey, so much suspicion and doubt and so many revelations. He had all the puzzle pieces now, or almost all of them, and they were assembled right in front of him, but the picture they formed was still obstructed from his view.

"We need to finish the video," he said definitively, thinking of Jenna. Where did she fit into all of this? Where did *he* fit into all of this? He needed to know what had happened that night.

"We'll start at the beginning, so Luke can see."

"No," Jason said. He sounded colder — stronger — than he ever had before. "There's no time." *We needed your help. There was no other way.* Max was still out there and so was Jenna. "Max knows I'm close."

Troy protested, and Rakesh backed Jason up.

"I'm not a moron," Luke finally said. Rakesh opened his mouth, but Jason kicked him before he could form the insult. "I want to see what happened." He crossed his arms across his chest, and so Sully pressed PLAY.

"Max, don't," Lacey said, and a thin arm reached for her. She pushed him back.

"I'll put the video on Facebook. What do you think Luke will do when he sees what you did with his best bro? Do you think Jenna will understand why you went behind her back? Everyone will know what a liar you are. I'm giving you a chance. I'll keep your secret. I'm not even asking that much in return."

They were watching something awful: the murder of an innocent girl, yet Jason's heart leapt. Jenna didn't know about Lacey and Troy. Jenna wasn't involved in Lacey's death.

Faintly, they heard a door creaking and the clamor of voices.

"Oh, hey, Lacey, what are you doing up here?" It was a girl's voice, friendly.

"Just, uh, looking for a bathroom," Lacey answered, her eyes nervously creeping to the side. Max must have ducked out of sight.

Luke was rapt, his expression pained. Jason tried to put himself in his shoes, observing his sister minutes before she died, powerless to warn her how dangerous the person she was protecting was.

"Rox told me no one was supposed to be up here. But you can use the one in her parents' room over there. The line downstairs is so annoying."

"Thanks, Laura."

A minute went by. "This is over, Max," Lacey hissed. "I'm not gonna go out with you. Tell the entire school about Troy for all I care. The worst part is I defended you to him. I actually *liked* you."

"I thought you were special. But you're just like every other conformist at this stupid school." A hand reached to her chest and yanked at the necklace hanging there, tearing the chain. "You think this means something?"

"Hey! Give that back!"

She disappeared from the frame, and as the five boys stared at a blurry wall, they heard the sounds of a struggle, and a girl's muffled shriek, and then nothing. A few minutes later, they could see someone's legs passing by the camera, and then nothing, until the picture went dead.

No one spoke. They sat staring at the screen, shell-shocked, the sounds of ragged breath filling the room, and then suddenly they were all talking — then shouting — at once.

"You had this video the whole time!"

"Why didn't you just tell me . . ."

"You let her hang out with that guy!"

". . . should never have trusted him."

"What are you even doing here?"

"I never *let* her do anything."

"My sister . . ."

"When I get my hands on him . . ."

"I loved her, too."

It was Rakesh who put a stop to it. "Shut up!" he screamed. "You're all giving me a headache. Jason, what do we do now?"

To Jason's surprise, they all looked at him expectantly. He wanted to tell them he couldn't help. He was tired and sore, spent. There had been too much risk already, too many twists, and for what? Lacey was still gone. And then he remembered. Jenna. Max was out there, and Jenna didn't know how dangerous he was. They could protect her. *He* could.

"We have to call the police," Jason said.

"I can handle Max Anderson," Luke replied, balling up his fists.

Jason already had his phone out of his pocket. It was a few minutes past one in the morning. Jenna's voice mails now seemed urgent, just like she'd been trying to tell him.

Troy and Sully reasoned with Luke as Jason checked his messages. The blood drained from his face when he heard Jenna's whispered plea.

"I should never have lied to you. I think there's something wrong with Max. *Please* call me back when you get this."

She had gone to Max. When Jason had not listened to her, she had gone to him, and now whatever happened to her would be his fault.

"I'm calling 911. Now. Someone find me Max's address." It was as if he'd been given superpowers; everyone listened to him. Luke stopped arguing, and Rakesh planted himself in front of the computer.

When the operator answered, he cleared his throat. "I'd like to report a murder," he said. If he hadn't been so focused on protecting Jenna, he would have savored the dramatic effect. As it was, Rakesh snorted.

"Sir, are you in any immediate danger?"

"Yeah. No. I mean, my friend is."

"What is your location?"

"My location? No, I'm fine. It's my friend. She's in danger."

"Sir, can you give me the address?"

He squinted over Rakesh's shoulder and recited Max's address.

There was a long pause. "You think this is real funny, huh?"

"What? What are you talking about? My friend is in danger!"

"Young man, do you know it's a crime to call in false reports?"

"No! This isn't a false report." He was growing more high-pitched and childlike with everything he said. He cupped a hand over the mouthpiece and asked Rakesh if he was sure it was the right address.

"Yeah, that's definitely his house," Troy answered. "I dropped Lacey off there a bunch of times."

"Have you ever heard of the boy who cried wolf?" the operator was asking sternly.

"I'm not crying wolf! Why don't you believe me?"

"But you were the first seven times you called in a threat to that address? Mr. Anderson has informed us he will be pressing charges if the harassment continues."

Max. He'd gotten to them first. Jason lowered the phone and ended the call. The group stood there staring at him quizzically. They were waiting for an explanation, for guidance. What was he going to tell them? That he'd been outplayed? That Max was smarter — and crazier — than any of them had realized?

"Well," he said, as authoritatively as he could muster, "I guess we're going with Plan B."

CHAPTER 29

*P*lan B involved arguing about who was going to drive (they settled on Luke because his car was the biggest), and then, briefly, about who was riding shotgun (Jason forced Rakesh to let Troy have it even though he conceded that, by the rules of shotgun, Rakesh had won the seat).

Jason was loath to admit it, but one thing Plan B did not involve was an actual plan, or rather, it was lacking a unified *plan*. They were agreed on the first step: Go to Max's. It was after this that their ideas diverged. Jason was planning to rescue Jenna. Luke was planning to rip Max's head off when they got there. Troy was planning to stop Luke from committing a felony. Rakesh was planning to not miss any action. Sully was planning to record whatever went down and post the video to YouTube, but Troy stared him down when he tried to squeeze his stocky frame into the Jeep, and they left him behind on the curb.

Jason attempted to concentrate on Jenna's voice mails as Luke whipped around the curves of Brighton's narrow streets.

"I never meant to lie to you. We didn't know what to do. I'll explain everything, but you have to talk to me. *Please* call me back."

"Ugh, turn on your phone! Call me back!"

"Okay, last message, but you should see how people look at Max at school. We needed someone else if anyone was going to

228

believe what Troy did to Lacey. I loved her, but I didn't know how much I would like or care about you, and I never wanted you to get hurt."

"Sorry, I lied about not leaving any more messages. Look, I'm going over to Max's. He got a new lead on Troy and he thinks we have enough to go to the police. I really want you on our side for this, so please, please, please call me back."

And then, the final hushed warning: "There's something wrong with Max."

Jenna had left that one just half an hour before. Through pursed lips, he asked how far away they were. "Halfway there," Troy answered. She had to be okay.

He dialed her number, but it rang through to voice mail. He tried again, and this time someone picked up on the third ring.

"Hello, Jason." It was Max, the soothing beats of the XX playing in the background.

"Max, uh, hi. Is Jenna with you?"

"Oh, she's right here, but she can't come to the phone right now, on account of I don't think it's a very good idea for you two to be talking. You never know what crazy theories you might come up with." The flat, emotionless delivery gave the words a sharp edge, and Jason tried to keep panic from setting in.

"Max, is Jenna alright?"

"I'm gonna take good care of Jenna. You don't need to worry about a thing."

And then there was a click as the line went dead.

"Any way we could drive a little faster?" Jason asked Luke through clenched teeth. The speedometer read fifty-two mph. Rakesh, rarely one for physical contact with other guys, gave his shoulder a comforting squeeze.

Max's house was dark when they pulled up outside. Luke jumped out first, followed closely by Troy, who restrained him by the back of his shirt.

"Dude, what are you gonna do?"

"I'm going to kill that guy."

"Buddy, I know you don't want to hear this, but that gets us nowhere good. Jason, what's our angle?"

He swallowed. "I heard music when we talked. Max said he uses his garage as a studio. That's probably where he has Jenna. If we can get in there, we can try to reason with him." He didn't add that the studio was probably soundproof, and so if Jenna was screaming no one would be able to hear, or that the cold-hearted, calculating person he'd just spoken to on the phone didn't seem much inclined to reason with anyone. They had to start somewhere.

Be okay, be okay, please be okay, Jason soundlessly repeated the mantra to himself as they filed up the driveway. How could he have let this happen? Why hadn't he seen the truth? They could see the tiniest sliver of light below the closed entrance to the garage, but it was otherwise unyielding. Troy led them along the side, into the narrow space between the freestanding wall and a hedge. Still without speaking, Rakesh gestured to the window set above all of their heads. The next thing Jason knew, Troy was hoisting his entire body up to look through it.

When he saw Jenna, he wanted to cheer. She was alive! But it only took a minute to realize alive and safe were not the same thing. Her wrists were bound and she was crying. He followed her line of vision to where Max was standing, leaning toward her. Jason surveyed the rest of the room. On the table next to him was a chain saw — he wouldn't even have to move to pick it up. He gestured down to Troy, who lowered him to the ground.

"Okay," he whispered. "Jenna's in there. I don't think he's hurt her yet, but he's got her tied up. And he's got a chain saw, so there's that."

"How do we get in?" Luke asked.

"There's a door against the back wall, just around that corner. But we can't let him lay a hand on Jenna."

Before any of them could stop him, Luke had rushed around the corner. They heard him yank the door open. Troy followed in his path, but Jason and Rakesh pulled him backward before he could reach the entrance.

"Did you not hear me? It's like *The Texas Chainsaw Massacre* in there, and we know what he's capable of."

"I ride with Luke."

"Then he'll kill both of you. If you want to help him, we can't be stupid."

Rakesh silenced them both with a finger to his lips. Luke had entered the garage, leaving the door slightly ajar, and now they could faintly hear what was going on inside.

"Hello, Luke." That deadly calm again. Jason held his breath, sweating.

Luke's roar was animal and raw, but midway through it was interrupted by a buzzing crackle, transforming from anger to pain, and mixing with the sounds of Jenna shrieking. Troy bolted for the door too quickly for them to stop him, but to Jason's relief he stopped at the corner, merely peeking through the cracked door. Jason rubbed his hands together nervously, desperate to know what was happening inside.

"Feeling limber?" he asked Rakesh, raising an eyebrow toward the window.

Rakesh grunted as he lifted Jason up. "One of these days I'm going to stop carrying you on my shoulders. Then where will you be?"

Jason's retort was left unspoken when he saw Luke curled on the ground, groaning. A few steps away, Max was duct taping Jenna's mouth shut. She was whimpering, and her eyes were trained on something Jason didn't recognize in Max's left hand.

He looked over at Troy. "Is that a . . ."

"Yeah, Taser."

Rakesh, whose arms had begun to shake, lowered Jason down to the ground. "Why am I not surprised that guy has a Taser?"

"They only hold a couple charges." Troy had come back to huddle with them.

"And why am I not surprised this guy knows all about them?"

Jason ignored him, addressed himself directly to Troy. "What are you saying?"

Weakly, Rakesh joked, "Yo, I am not getting tased, bro."

None of them cracked a smile.

"Look, I don't think any of us have to get tased, but if two or more of us go in there at once, we can overpower him."

"Except for the chain saw."

"So we have to make sure one of us gets to the chain saw first."

From inside, they could hear Max's hollow, maniacal laugh. "What's the matter, Gray? Not so tough now, are we?" It was followed by the rip of duct tape being torn. Luke was going to be of no use to them if they got inside. "I guess you've figured it out by now? How your *boy* was dating your sister right under your nose? It was so obvious! But I guess that's where I came in. Lacey thought I'd be so happy to cover for her. Like pretending to hang out with her was the best thing that could ever happen to me. Your sister was kind of a brat, did you know that?" Luke grunted, and they heard the thud of Max kicking him.

Jason kept one ear on what Max was saying as he tried to focus on Troy's plot to get into the garage. "Jason, you'll go first. You have to distract him."

He nodded, but Rakesh must have seen his doubt, because he cut in. "I'll go first."

"No, Rock, you don't have to."

"You got the crap beaten out of you yesterday. . . ."

"So did you!"

"Well, for one thing, I'm tougher, and for another, Luke didn't repeatedly punch me in the face. If the psychopath in there tries to tase you, you're screwed. I, however, am quick like a cat, or a fox, or a panther. . . ."

Jason felt a rush of gratitude for his friend, but Troy was less amused. "We get it. Fine, you'll go first. Get him to turn his back to the door, and then, Jason, you grab the chain saw; I'll tackle Max."

"And then Jason can rescue Jenna," Rakesh said suggestively.

Jason felt himself blush in the darkness, and he was glad Troy ignored him. "We'll go on my count. Okay?"

Inside, Max had turned his attention to Jenna. "You couldn't just leave it alone. You think your BFF cared about you?" His calm was beginning to fray around the edges, and now he was practically spitting the words. "I knew more about her than you did. I knew more about her than *anyone*. You're just like her, you know that?"

Through her taped mouth, Jason couldn't hear a response, but he knew they couldn't wait much longer. He felt a resigned sense of dread, like Hamlet at the beginning of the fifth act. The instant the play popped into his head, Jason saw the parallels. Everyone undone by mistrust and treachery, minor conflicts blossoming into full-blown blood feuds, a pile of bodies on the floor. Was that how this was going to end? It occurred to him that that was what Max wanted, and he felt a surge of anger. He had killed Lacey, torn a huge gaping hole in everyone's world, just because he was unhappy. Jason wasn't going to give him the chance to do the same to Luke and Jenna.

"Yeah," Jason said finally. "Rakesh, don't get tased, okay? Troy, tackle him before he gets near Rock. Ready?"

As stealthily as they could, they crept to the corner of the garage, ducking back behind the wall when they were bathed in light from the open door. Rakesh stood at the front, and Troy held up his hand, silently mouthing, "One . . . two . . . three." As soon as the third finger went up, Rakesh shot off, piercing the night with a battle cry so loud and surprising it startled even Jason. But a moment later he was following at his friend's heels and crouching at the door so Troy could see in over his head. The garage was smaller than Jason had realized from the window — there wasn't really anywhere for Rakesh to go. But Max was caught off guard all the same, spinning away from Jenna to see where the noise was coming from. Rakesh was a flurry of motion, jumping over the recovering Luke and from corner to corner. Confusion washed over Max when he realized who the second intruder was. "What the —" he muttered, and then looked down at the Taser in his hand and grinned, as if realizing for the first time that he had a weapon.

"What you gonna do, freak?" Rakesh taunted as he bounced into the corner farthest from the door. "Trust me, you could play me your latest acoustic song, and it would hurt me worse than that toy in your hand."

Jason darted in once Max's back was fully turned, heading directly for the chain saw. Maybe his feet fell as heavily as they felt, or maybe something in Rakesh's behavior gave him away, but Max whipped around again and charged right for him. Jason was at the chain saw first, tugging inexpertly at the starter cord. He was expecting the motor to roar, but there was nothing. He pulled again, harder this time, and Max threw back his head and laughed. He was three steps away, Taser arm outstretched. There was nowhere for Jason to go. He wanted to shut his eyes. Instead he forced himself to look at Jenna. He'd seen how scared she was before. She had to know he wasn't going to let anything happen to her. But Jenna was gone from her chair. Just before the Taser made contact, Max crumpled to the ground, and the garage filled with an awful, mechanical wail. Jenna stood before Jason, where Max had been a second before. In her duct-taped hands was the electric guitar she had used to crack Max over the head.

CHAPTER 30

Max came to as they waited for the police to arrive. Rakesh had called them while Jason untied Jenna and Troy helped Luke to his feet. Max was conscious but groggy, and Troy quickly taped his hands behind his back and hovered over him in case he got any ideas. Rakesh wasn't taking no for an answer from the police this time.

"Maybe you didn't hear me, this is John Sullivan the *third*," he said very clearly. Jason would have gone with fourth, but Rakesh was selling it. "Perhaps you know my father, John Sullivan? Yeah, he's the guy who plays golf with your boss on Saturdays, and if you don't send a squad car over here right now, I will make sure the mayor himself knows you were the one responsible for ignoring my calls about an *actual murderer*."

"I'm sorry," Jenna said as soon as Jason had ripped the tape from her lips. "I should never have lied to you. I shouldn't have trusted Max. I'm sorry I got you involved in this whole mess."

"You're the one who just saved my life, I should be thanking you."

She kept talking as if he hadn't said anything. "Messaging you, pretending to be Lacey, it was Max's idea. He showed me that video of Troy, and I didn't know . . . I thought . . . He said Troy had killed Lacey, but he couldn't prove it. It made sense. I mean, she never lied to me, but here was this huge secret. I was the one who went into her Facebook. When I found your message, Jason,

236

I just lost it. It was like you were everyone who was never going to get a chance to get to know Lacey. But then Max thought maybe you could help us, and that's why I wrote you."

She started to cry, great, heaving sobs she couldn't speak through. Jason put his arms around her, letting her weep onto his shoulder. He still had so many questions.

Though he looked a little worse for the wear, Luke was standing now. He stumbled toward Max, and Troy steadied him. "He's not worth it," he said. From the look in his eyes, Jason wasn't sure he meant it.

They heard sirens in the distance, and Jason knew it was his only chance to find out the thing he couldn't find out for himself. He poked Max's shoulder until he cast his dark eyes up to him.

"Why me?"

"You messaged her first."

"No. I don't buy that. You had everything you needed to frame Troy. Why get me involved? Besides, I can't be the only person who messaged her."

Max smiled. It sent a chill down Jason's spine. "You were so easy," he said at last. "The music you like, the photos of your boring suburban life, the way no one notices you. You're just like me. I knew exactly how you were going to react, exactly what you were going to do. It was like finding a puppet."

Jenna had drawn away and was wiping her eyes with a tissue. Jason stepped forward so he was right above Max. "Did you know I was going to do this?" he asked sweetly. He pulled back his foot and kicked him as hard as he could in the side. Then he walked out of the garage.

*   *   *

The rest of the night passed in a blur. The postmidnight excursions and sleepless nights caught up with Jason all at once, and a fog descended on him. He watched as the police led Max away in handcuffs. At some point paramedics arrived and even though Jenna and Luke both waved them off, they were loaded into an ambulance and driven away. Jason didn't know how much time passed before he found himself at the station house, sitting in a windowless interrogation room, a grizzled detective who'd introduced himself as Officer O'Leary opposite him. Jason answered every question posed to him, allowing all the secrets and lies to fall away for the first time in what felt like forever. When he finished the story, his head felt like a ton of bricks.

O'Leary whistled quietly. "Sheesh," he said. "My day, you get a girl's number, you ask her out. Maybe she says she's gotta wash her hair and you see her at the dance with another guy, you get your heart a little broken. But I tell ya, I don't envy you kids with your Facebook, your YouTube. It's hard enough to meet someone you can be yourself around without all these identities getting in the way."

Jason stared at him blankly, but his mind flashed to Jenna, the night in the car outside Troy's house. How easy it had been, how natural. It was strange to think she'd been the one he'd been falling for all along. How many hours ago had he discovered Lacey's profile on her computer? Everything seemed so black-and-white at that moment, but here, in the fuzzy light of exhaustion and revelation, Jason wasn't so sure. It was strange to think Jenna was the one he'd been falling for the whole time. The one who'd written the messages that made his breath shorten and his heart jump. All the secrets were finally out in the open, but there were some things he still couldn't get clear.

"C'mon, kid," Office O'Leary said after he didn't answer. "Let's get you home. One thing the Internet hasn't changed is how much one of those hurts." He gestured to Jason's bruised and swollen eye. Jason blinked, and as if on cue, waves of pain reverberated through his head, causing him to wince.

"Thanks," he managed, as the gruff, graying man helped him to his feet.

By the time he stepped outside the station, the sun was rising. Rakesh was sitting in the front seat of Mrs. Adams's car, and Jason could tell from her expression that she was right in the middle of one of her epic tirades, but she paused, mouth agape, when Rakesh spotted Jason and waved him over. He tumbled into the backseat, dazed from the daylight.

"Oh, Jason, you must be so tired. I'll take you straight home." Her voice was thick with concern. If he weren't so numb from the wild events of the past twenty-four hours, he would have marveled at the rare occasion when Rakesh was in trouble for something while his involvement would go unpunished. He had no idea how Rakesh had convinced the police not to call his mother, but he was deeply grateful. He thought his brain might sputter out if he had to go through the whole story again.

The next thing he knew, Mrs. Adams was shaking him gently. "Sweetie, we're at your house." Her face loomed above him, and he lurched backward, startled before he realized he'd fallen asleep against the window. "Are you sure you don't want to come over and sleep in the guest bedroom for a little while?

Rocky says your mom will be home soon, but I don't want to leave you alone."

"No, it's fine," he said. The words felt heavy as they passed through his gravelly throat. "I just want my bed." He sounded like a cranky toddler, but he didn't care.

When he got upstairs, he reflexively planted himself at his desk chair and logged in to Facebook. When his screen lit up with the missed messages from Jenna, he felt his body sag a little.

"What am I doing?" he mumbled. Officer O'Leary had been right: There was nothing more than confusion waiting for him online. So he shut down his computer, turned off his phone, and fell into a deep, dreamless sleep.

EPILOGUE:
SIX WEEKS LATER

oes she know that's what you're wearing?" Rakesh couldn't mask his skepticism. He sat on Jason's bed in a narrowly cut black suit.

"She won't care," Jason answered without taking his eyes off his reflection. He'd found the tuxedo T-shirt in a thrift shop months ago and bought it even though at the time he was vehemently anti–school dance. But here he was, about to get into a limo that would take him to a darkened gym where a DJ would no doubt be blasting LFMAO and Ke$ha. If there was anything he'd learned, it was that things didn't usually work out the way you expected.

"So she *doesn't* know?"

"Does Meg know you're wearing a tie so skinny I think it might be anorexic?"

"Adrian Grenier wore this tie to his last movie premiere."

"The guy from *Entourage*? Is that supposed to be a selling point?"

"Jason, it's a first impression. Which means you have to *impress* her."

"It's not a first impression," Jason protested. "We've hung out before."

"Yeah, but not on a date. Don't you think it will be weird enough without your hipster wardrobe choices?"

Jason didn't answer. He couldn't deny it was weird that he and Jenna were going on a date. He had flirted with her before, but that was when he thought she was Lacey. When they first became friends, there was a small spark, but it was buried beneath his devotion to Lacey — and then extinguished completely by Jenna's betrayal. But the weirdest part about tonight was that Jason *wasn't* nervous.

In the days after Max's arrest, Jason had wandered around in a fog of grief and sadness. The girl he'd fallen in love with was gone forever — worse than that, the girl he'd fallen for was an invention of a murderer and brought to life by someone he thought was his friend.

At school, Jason was no longer invisible. Lacey's story had circulated like the plague, developing twisted strains with each retelling — Rakesh recounted one version he had heard that involved Jason wielding nunchucks to knock a gun from Max's hands. Of course Rakesh had no problem inflating his own heroics, and he made sure to correct any recount that didn't properly recognize his athleticism or bravery. Kids in the hall looked at Jason with newfound respect, but he was so lost in his own thoughts he barely noticed, let alone cared. He stayed off Facebook and e-mail, and rarely checked his phone, and messages from classmates he barely knew inviting him to parties or offering a shoulder to cry on all went unanswered. And then just as everything was beginning to settle down, he came home to find a thick envelope, his name etched across the front in round neat letters, the return address one "J. Merrick."

He was the first one home that day, and his stomach somersaulted when he found the letter in the hall beneath the mail slot. He smuggled it up to his room unopened and laid it carefully on the bed, looking down at it anxiously, as if it might explode in his face at any minute. The wanting to know, the not wanting to know — he hadn't felt like this since Lacey. Who was Jenna. Who had sent the letter that was in front of him now. Finally, he ripped the envelope open.

Dear Jason,
I can't tell you how many times I started this note – there are like 12 tabs in my browser open with e-mails and messages to you. If I could figure out how smoke signals work, I'd probably try to contact you that way too. I wanted to write you before I figured out what Max did, and even more after. I have so much to say, and I don't know how to say any of it, so let me start with this:

I'M SORRY.
I'm sorry I pretended to be Lacey, I'm sorry I lied to you, I'm sorry I almost got you killed by Max, I'm sorry I haven't written you before now, I'm sorry I ruined everything, I'm sorry about everything. Actually, wait, that's not true. There's one thing I'm not sorry about. I'm not sorry I met you.
What I did was wrong – it was crazy and it was stupid, and if I'd known how

dangerous it was, I would never have let
Max talk me into it. I don't expect you—
or anyone—to understand, but I loved
Lacey so much. She was like my sister,
and when she died, I lost a part of
myself so big I felt like I would never
heal. And the thing I couldn't get over
was that her death didn't make any sense.
I had so many questions: What was she
doing on the balcony? How could someone
just fall off? Why wasn't anyone acknowl-
edging how messed up everything was? And
then I ran into Max at Sam's one day, and
he asked me how I'd been. Everyone had
been tiptoeing around this horrible thing
that happened, and he was the first person who said Lacey's name aloud instead
of whispering it like even the word Lacey
was some shameful secret, and I just lost
it. He let me sit in his car and cry and
he was the only one who would listen to
me when I said I thought something terrible had happened, something no one was
talking about.

Of course, now I know why, and it makes
me sick to my stomach to think about how
much I trusted him, how much LACEY trusted
him, and how evil he was. He was the one
who told me about Troy, and as soon as he
did, I wanted to go to the police, but

he said no one would believe it. He said
we had to prove it. It was his idea to
hack into Lacey's Facebook account, and
if I hadn't been so devastated, I would
have realized how insane it all was, but
everything was already so mixed up that
it seemed like a good idea. So we did.
When we found your message, he said you'd
be perfect, and I believed him.
This is going to sound crazy, Jason, I
know, but when I pretended to be Lacey,
it was like she was still alive, like I
still had her in my life. I don't expect
you to forgive me, but I need you to
understand, everything I did was out of
love for her. I felt like I had my friend
back. And then I started getting to know
you–technically, I guess, Lacey did–and
that's when I started to realize it wasn't
going to work out the way I wanted to.
Because while I was pretending to be
Lacey, I was starting to like you. Like
like you. But I couldn't do that to my
best friend–even though "my best friend"
was me pretending to be my best friend–
and I knew you'd never forgive me once
you found out the truth. And I didn't
even know what the truth was anymore.
You'd send me these videos and when I'd
write back, I'd be sending you MY

response, not the one I imagined her
having. Suddenly this thing that had
seemed so necessary and sensible seemed
like the nightmare that it was.

That day that you found her profile at my
house I was scared about what you were
going to do, but I was relieved because I
didn't have to lie to you anymore. Lying
to you was the worst part.

I still have so much more to say, but
this is too long already. So let me just
say one more time I'm so, so sorry. And
thank you for saving my life. It's like I
said, I don't expect you to forgive me—
I don't think I'll ever forgive
myself—but I needed you to know this
stuff, because I also couldn't forgive
myself if I didn't tell you how special
I think you are and how much I care
about you.

Yours,

Jenna

PS: I'm sorry I stole your song (poem?).
But it was good. Really good. PLEASE keep
writing.

When Jason was finished reading, he sat very still. He was waiting for the anger to flare up inside him, to feel the sting of Jenna's deception anew. But to his surprise, the only thing he felt was warmth flooding his chest. He realized he was smiling.

For the first time, he had some clarity. And Jenna liked him. *Like* liked him.

He sat down at his computer and began to type.

You're the one who saved my life.

As soon as he'd sent the IM to Jenna, the familiar anticipation of waiting for a response crept into his body — his chest ping-ponging, his stomach flip-flopping, all of it vaguely pleasant.

Jason

It had begun with two little words with Lacey, and this time it only took one.

In the days and weeks that followed, they slipped into an easy correspondence, writing and IM'ing frequently. They mostly avoided the topic of Lacey, but not always — Jenna told him how Troy and Luke had been different in school, nicer to strangers they passed in the hall, more respectful of kids in their classes. Jason told her how he sometimes had nightmares about Max, but he left out the scariest part, which was that he was unable to rescue her.

"So when are we going to hang out?" Jenna asked when they were Skyping illicitly one night. Jason had been grounded ever since his mom had come home to find him bloodied and bruised and fresh from a trip to the police station. She was so shocked when he first recounted everything that happened that she punished him indefinitely, but lately she'd eased up, allowing him to use his computer for non-school-related things and not pestering him when he hung out with Rakesh after school.

"There's this dance," Jason answered.

"Jason Moreland, are you telling me you're going to spend a night in a gym decorated with cheesy plastic palm trees listening to Top 40?"

"I am if you are," he answered, trying to mask how desperately he hoped she'd say yes.

"Yes! But only if you promise me you'll actually dance."

"We'll see about that," he laughed, but even then he knew if it was important to Jenna he'd do it.

When Jason told Rakesh his mom had granted him permission to go and he'd secured a date, Rakesh whooped with joy and then quickly booked a limo and assembled a group. Before he headed off to his first school dance, Jason checked himself in the mirror one last time. For a brief moment, his mind bounced reflexively to Lacey. Instead of wondering about her approval, though, Jason felt an overwhelming sense of sadness for the dances she would not attend, the nights out she'd never enjoy. But he shook those thoughts from his head, and surveyed the face before him. The bruises had faded entirely, and his hair wasn't too floppy. For once the light wasn't bouncing off his glasses. Part of him wanted to snap a photo to post to Facebook, but the only person he wanted to impress wouldn't be checking her news feed — instead, she'd be hanging out with Jason.

Ruth Baron has worked as an editor at *O, The Oprah Magazine* and *Details*. She grew up in Philadelphia, lives in Brooklyn, and thinks about deleting her Facebook account every day.